MISTASIA

NOVELLAS

WHIZZENMOG BETRAYAL

&

GRACE'S QUEST

To my daughters, hoping we will soon begin to create stories together.

[1. Fantasy – Fiction. 2. Science Fiction – Fiction. 3. Wizards – Fiction. 4. Heroes – Fiction.]

Released in United States of America
Paperback format
First Edition, June 2014

DEAR READER!

Whizzenmog Betrayal is the first novella in the *Land of Mistasia* storyline. It takes place prior to *Land of Mistasia* (book 1). It is a story told by Ethan Whizzenmog about his life and struggle to fit into the proud and powerful Whizzenmog family of wizards.

In this story; long ago, Mistasia was peaceful and protected by the Whizzenmog family of wizards. Ethan and Rainer Whizzenmog were the next generation being trained by their father to protect Cadieux Castle and its royal family.

Ethan struggled with his powers while his brother Rainer excelled. Feeling weak and useless, the young wizard turned to a powerful sorcerer for guidance, Pierre LaCroiux.

Ethan found himself growing stronger and more confident in his new powers, but he soon would discover a betrayal that would lead him to choose between family and sorcery.

I hope you enjoy this novella.

Sincerely,

Christopher M. Purrett (Author)

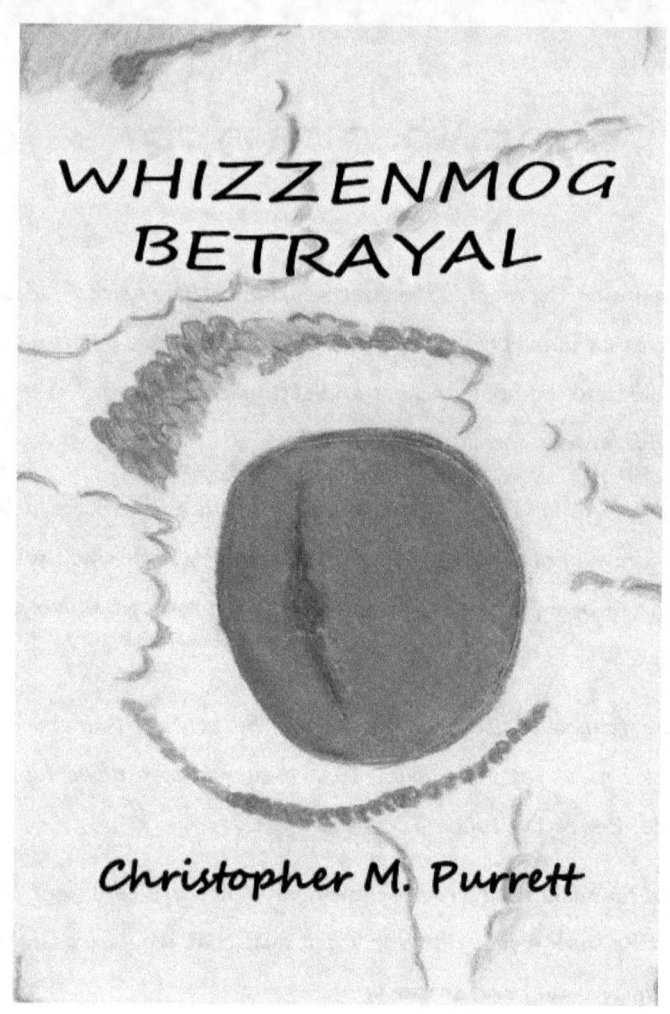

WHIZZENMOG BETRAYAL

Christopher M. Purrett

www.LandofMistasia.com

www.Purrett.com

CHAPTERS

ETHAN WHIZZENMOG

<u>1</u>

Standing before me was the shadowy figure of my brother. His back was to the light of the full moon, which hung large in the dark, star-filled sky. His usually red-colored fur was nearly black. His eyes were intense and fixed on me.

My heart pounded in my chest. It was hard to breathe. I held my arm outstretched with my wand gripped tightly in my right paw. My yellow fur seemed to glow against the brightness of the full moon making it quite difficult to hide.

"Don't do it, Rainer!" I pleaded as the tip of his wand lit up. "No!" I screamed in fear.

A bolt of light dashed toward me and slammed into my chest before I could jump out of the way. My body went numb and I fell on my back. I was now staring into the Mistasian night sky. The blades of grass wrapped around my long fox ears. I wanted to get up and run away, but nothing moved. My big brother had just paralyzed me with a spell. It was the same thing every time. We would begin to practice our spells and one way or another it would end with me losing.

"Great job, Rainer. You have really developed into a premier wizard, son." The voice of our father, Glyndon Whizzenmog, proudly proclaimed. "The King and Queen will be truly impressed with your skills."

"Thank you, father!" my brother gleefully replied.

"Tomorrow I will present you to the King. You are ready to join me in protecting the throne, Rainer."

Then our father turned his attention to me as I still remained motionless in the cool grass. "Ethan. I'm disappointed," He said with a deep exhale. "Your brother has defeated you with the exact same spell three days in a row now. Will you ever learn?"

Even in the dark, I could see the disapproval in my father's eyes. Rainer was so much stronger and quicker than me. It was unfair. We weren't the same wizard.

I watched as my father patted my brother on the back, "Great job!" Then he turned and walked away leaving me paralyzed in the grass.

My heart sank. I don't know why it still bothered me...my father had always been that way. He was embarrassed of me.

Rainer pointed his wand at my chest again. It lit up sending a warmth surging through my body as if the blood suddenly flowed through my veins again. I took a deep breath. When my brother reached out his hand to help me, I pushed it away.

"I don't want your help!" I shouted in disgust. "Why do you have to do that?" I angrily yelled at him once I was back to my feet.

Rainer was taller than I was too. I had to stand on my tip toes to see eye to eye with him.

"Cut that out, Ethan." Rainer shoved me in the chest and laughed. I stumbled backwards and tripped over a rock, falling back into the grass again. Rainer quickly realized he had pushed too hard.

"Hey, I'm sorry. Let me help you up."

"I don't need your help, brother!" I was fuming. My left paw was bruised, but not as deeply as my ego. He just didn't understand what it was like to feel small...weak. I wanted to show him so badly, but knew I would never match up to him...our father's favorite son.

"Come on. Let's go back to the house." Rainer turned and started walking, but then stopped when he noticed I wasn't following. He was used to me following him everywhere. I had always been envious of him, but now I was just angry. "Ethan?"

"You go," I calmly replied. "I want to be alone."

"But father is waiting for us?" Rainer ignorantly stated.

"No, Rainer." I held back tears. "Just you!"

WOLVERINE FOREST

2

The air was crisp and cool as it swept across Dragon Lake and floated into Cadieux Village. I started to walk along the shore just thinking to myself and not really paying attention to the village behind me in the distance. When I finally stopped to pick up a crescent-shaped rock at my foot and toss it into the lake I noticed the torches from the village were no longer visible.

Should I go back?, I questioned myself.

"No," I answered aloud and tossed the rock into the lake. "They'll never notice I'm gone."

So I continued to walk along the shore. Dragon Lake was the calmest water anywhere in Mistasia. It looked like it was frozen as the moonlight reflected from the top of the steady water. In the distance I could make out the treetops of Wolverine Forest.

Why is he so mean to me? Images of my father's disappointed expression haunted me all night long. The farther I got from the castle, the more I realized I could never go back. There was no reason for me to return.

I should just keep walking, I thought to myself. Behind me I heard a snort. When I turned, I gasped.

Staring at me was a very large wolverine. The beast growled. Its fangs hung down from its upper lip. The Wolverine had snuck up on me. I could hear my father's voice, "You will never learn!"

Suddenly, I realized I had my wand in my paw and pointed it at the beast. The Wolverine grunted loudly and bent down to attack.

"No, don't do it!" I yelled in my deepest voice, which sounded more like a whimpering child.

The wolverine charged. I fired the first spell I could think of in a panic. It completely missed because my hand was shaking so badly. The spell hit a small tree causing it to drop all its leaves and acorns, leaving it naked. I ducked to avoid the wolverine, but it still grabbed me. Now, I was dangling in the air by my ankles. I dropped my wand, which the beast quickly snapped up from the grass. It pushed its big, ugly face into mine. Its warm, smelly breath burned my nostrils.

I'm in so much trouble. I cried in my head. I hoped this hungry beast wasn't going to eat me for a snack. I closed my eyes. Then, we were moving again. When I opened them I realized the wolverine was running back toward the forest. Where there were more wolverines!

I hit the ground with a thud, rubbing my neck as it throbbed with pain. Then, I heard a voice that would change my life.

"What brings a Whizzenmog to the Wolverine Forest?" The crass voice challenged me.

I hesitated to look up and see who was speaking.

"Answer me, fox!" He yelled.

I shuddered at the anger in his voice. It reminded me of my father. I tried to answer his question, but when I moved my lips nothing came out.

"Stubborn...just like his father!" The voice replied.

"No!" I suddenly found my voice. For the first time I looked away from the dirt-covered forest floor and saw the elven man that sat before me. He was old and thin. He had short white hair, and a long braided white beard. The elf glared at me. "I mean...I am not like my father." I clarified.

The man smiled and sat upright in his throne. It was a beautifully carved wooden throne made from the root of a massive tree. Two wolverines stood at his sides like guards.

"Who are you?" I mustered up the courage to ask.

The elf scoffed as though he was offended that I didn't know.

"My name is Pierre LaCroiux, and I ask you again young Whizzenmog. What brings you to my forest?"

"Well...I...well," I stammered as I tried to figure out how to explain my situation.

Then LaCroiux stood from his throne and walked toward me. My heart skipped a beat, and I had to remind myself to breathe. My paws trembled as I began to recoil. The elder elf put out his hand and placed it on my shoulder. Then he knelt before me. Our eyes met and a strange sensation overcame me. It was calm. My paws no longer trembled, my heartbeat returned to normal.

"You can tell me...Ethan," Pierre LaCroiux spoke in a friendly voice.

"How...how did you know my name?" I didn't know if I should be fearful or honored by his knowledge.

"I make it my business to know the names of the King's wizard guardians," he smiled. "Word has come to my ear that you and your father are...not seeing eye to eye." He suddenly stopped. He appeared to be awaiting my answer.

"Ah...yes Lord LaCroiux," I responded.

"Sorcerer," He corrected. "You have yet to explain why you have come to my forest, young Whizzenmog?"

"I was walking along Dragon Lake when I ran into one of your guards," I replied feeling silly. The guardian of the king would always be on his guard and not so easily captured by his foe.

"So you are my prisoner then?" LaCroiux chuckled. "A Whizzenmog wizard as my prisoner? Now that is something." His laughter became a roar as the Wolverines around him began to laugh with a raspy voice.

I felt a pit in my stomach.

"Do you really want to be my prisoner, Ethan?" The elven sorcerer questioned as he again knelt before me.

I shook my head no. I most definitely didn't want to be a sorcerer's prisoner.

"But you don't want to go back home either?"

"My father doesn't want me anyway. My family is better off without me." I replied in disgrace.

"Then you are welcome to stay here...in Wolverine Forest. I can teach you the way of a sorcerer. You will never again feel the shame your father has created in you. I can lead you to a greater purpose. You will become stronger than you ever dreamed possible."

I began to smile. I wanted so badly to be important. To be strong and powerful. Maybe sorcery was the way that I can be great?

"Yes." I responded. It was the quickest decision I had come to in my lifetime.

I remained in Wolverine Forest and became Sorcerer LaCroiux's apprentice. He showed me things that I never even dreamed possible. As a wizard your powers are limited to what you can do by your wand; however, as a sorcerer there seems to be no limitations. Whatever my mind can imagine I can conjure into reality...both beautiful and frightening.

I never felt so alive, and so powerful. Sorcery definitely had its advantages over wizardry. LaCroiux brought a twenty-foot tall tree to life. It pulled its roots from the ground and began walking around. The tree snatched up a wolverine and tossed it like a pebble. Another time, LaCroiux showed me how to control fire. He set fire to a small bush and then made the flames dance and stretch on his command, even making shapes out of the flames. He grabbed a sword right from the powerful grip of a Wolverine Soldier with the arm of a flame creature.

For the first time in my life I believed I could challenge my brother. He would be no match for my sorcery.

One windy night, I walked at the edge of the forest staring across Dragon Lake. I couldn't see Cadieux Castle, but I knew where it was in the distance. The moon was full this night and it reflected off the lake the same way it had the first night I arrived here. For a brief moment, I wondered if my father had even noticed that I was gone.

He has Rainer. My mind answered in a rage. It didn't matter whether I was there or not. A surge of anger overtook me and I snapped the branch from a nearby tree and flung it far across the lake. Dragon Lake swallowed it quickly with almost no wake in the water. A slight ripple rolled outward. I followed it with my eyes until it landed along the narrow sandy beach at my paws.

A noise came from behind me. I figured it was another wolverine. When I turned around there was no one.

I furrowed my brow. I knew that I had heard something. I reentered the forest and searched for what could have made the noise.

Footprints? In the dirt was a trail of footprints most definitely not wolverine in origin. I followed the prints through the winding and sometimes narrow spaces between the trees until they vanished at the base of a very wide tree trunk. I folded my arms across my chest.

Where did they go? Footprints don't just stop. There had to be an explanation. This forest was full of surprises. What happened next shouldn't have been so shocking. After walking around the tree a couple of times in frustration I again stopped next to the last set of footprints just in front of the tree. I stepped inside them, placing my paws exactly. The footprints were larger than mine. I stared at my paws for a few moments and exhaled deeply. Then I glanced up at the tree and noticed something new, a unique shape in the bark of the tree's trunk. It appeared to be a handle. I reached out and grabbed hold. Then the front of the tree swung open revealing a staircase leading up.

I moved inside and the door shut behind me. It was extremely dark. I used my paws along the wall to guide myself up the winding staircase. I worried that if I used my wand to light my way whoever had made those tracks would know that I had figured out my way inside. Finally, I reached another door. Light peeked out from around its frame. I could hear voices. One was very familiar...my teacher, Sorcerer LaCroiux, and the other sounded like someone I knew. I tried to place the voice.

"Do you believe that this is the way you want to resolve your issues with your brother?" I heard LaCroiux ask harshly.

Brother? I wondered. It couldn't be. **Rainer?**

The second voice responded, "My brother has held his position for too long. Together we can rid this kingdom of his ignorance."

Prince Cragon Cadieux? I was shocked.

"And when King Steven is gone, you will assume the throne?" Sorcerer LaCroiux crassly questioned. "I don't see how that is worth the trouble for me. What do I gain from this, Prince Cragon?"

"You would become my advisor. Live in the castle," the evil prince responded hoping to persuade the sorcerer to join his side. "You would no longer have to live in the wild with these animals," he said, referring to the wolverines.

"I want control over everything outside Cadieux Village," LaCroiux demanded.

"Everything? But..." Cragon sounded stunned at the request. "That sounds like a hefty request, friend."

The sinister sorcerer responded with a snicker, "So does asking me to eliminate the King and Queen."

Their conversation frightened me, so I quickly escaped from the hideout and dashed back into the forest toward my makeshift home in the base of a large hollow tree.

It wasn't long before Sorcerer LaCroiux returned. He glided across the forest floor like a ghost. His robe dragged along the dirt making it appear he had no feet.

"Ethan!" LaCroiux anxiously called. "Where are you? I have something to share with you."

I took a deep breath and stuck my head out from my home.

"Oh, there you are. Come here, Ethan." The sorcerer carried a wide smile upon his normally weary face.

That sent a shiver of fear down my spine. If the thought of eliminating the King and Queen made him happy, I wanted no part of making him unhappy.

"Ethan, we have a proposal from the Prince of Cadieux." LaCroiux twirled his braided beard in his fingers. His smile had increased.

My throat was so dry it hurt to swallow. I rubbed my paw across my wet nose nervously. "What is it?" I asked, careful not to reveal that I already knew the plan.

"How would you like to test your newly learned skills?" The sorcerer goaded.

"My skills?" I asked. The dryness in my throat had wiggled its way all the way down into my stomach, which now ached with each breath.

The elven sorcerer's eyes were piercing. It was like he could see straight through me, and knew just how to control me.

"Ethan." He softly whispered. Sorcerer LaCroiux looked around before he continued, as if he thought someone else would overhear, but the only other beasts in this forest were the Wolverines and they didn't speak so who would they tell what they heard?

"You were destined for this moment. The day you arrived at my throne crying for a purpose, wishing you were more than the son of a wizard. That was the day I gave you a purpose...power and sorcery. You can do so much more than your lowly brother. Ethan Whizzenmog, today is the day you make the choice to remain a meager wizard from the family that serves a weak King, or claim your place as a powerful and majestic sorcerer that stands by the side of the true and mighty ruler of Mistasia." Pierre LaCroiux reached out and placed his large, skeletal hand on my paw.

I felt the adrenaline surging through my fur. It reached the ends of my body. I inhaled sharply.

"Imagine it, Ethan. You're standing beside the throne of Cadieux, as your family bows at your feet."

A smirk invaded my once fear-driven face. The worries of the meeting between LaCroiux and Cragon Cadieux had vanished. A feeling of clarity had overcome me. It was my choice. I was here for a reason. I could have gone home at any time in the past, but I choose to stay here in Wolverine Forest with Sorcerer LaCroiux to teach me the dark powers of sorcery. I wasn't going back to a family that hated me...that thought I was inferior.

"I'll show them," I finally spoke.

LaCroiux stood tall at the opening to my new home in this secluded forest.

"So I guess that means you're looking to demonstrate your skills, apprentice?"

I quickly sprung into action. I heard the snap of a twig behind me and spun around. My arm swung out and across my body like a swinging sword. I felt it crash to a stop against the chest of a Wolverine. Lifting him up, I flung the heavy and muscular beast into the air and over my head with ease. It crashed to the forest floor with a sickening thud.

Sorcerer LaCroiux had an approving smile on this elderly face when I again met his glance.

"We need to begin to prepare!"

THE RETURN HOME

3

A cool breeze flowed through the Wolverine Forest, as the moonlight crept in with each gust. I knelt on the limb of a tree perched high atop the forest's edge overlooking Dragon Lake. On the far side of the lake, was Cadieux Castle. The sky glittered as millions of stars shown above the peaceful castle below. I had forgotten how mesmerizing the nighttime sky was in Mistasia. Lately, all I had seen was the deep-colored leaves of the Wolverine Forest hanging over my head like a cloud.

I had in my hand a small wooden cylinder given to me by Sorcerer LaCroiux; he called it a "magnifinder". It was his creation and it looked like a simple small branch except at one end was an opening. I held the contraption with the open end to my eye. The device allowed me to see a great distance; with it, Cadieux Castle was easily visible.

Day after day, I would return to the same position in the trees and watch the King's guards as they moved around the castle. My master, Pierre LaCroiux, had spoken of a mystical item that the King's guards would be transporting to the castle.

"King Steven's guards discovered an emerald," LaCroiux had revealed to me before sending me high into the trees where I now spent most of my time awaiting the moment I could catch a glimpse of them bringing it into the castle.

Emeralds were powerful jewels that allowed its beholder to wheeled great power. To have this green gemstone would give them the power to rule all of Mistasia. If this was an emerald, it would be the last of its kind and extremely valuable.

In the early dawn, I began to dose. My yellow furry head grew heavy. I leaned against the tree trunk and slowly closed my eyes. I just wanted to sleep a few moments...I was so tired. Relaxation began to sweep through my body as all my tired and sore muscles released the night's tension. It felt great.

My eyes suddenly opened wide as I felt myself slipping. I gripped the tree branch that had been under me as I fell. Now, I found myself hanging extremely high in the air dangling above an obstacle course of branches that would batter me to a bloodied pulp if I let go. With all my strength, I pulled myself up.

Holding the branch tightly, I attempted to regain my composure. My heart was still racing and I felt sweat on my brow.

"The magnifinder!" I shouted as I realized it was gone. If I dropped it, it would surely be destroyed. "LaCroiux is gonna kill me," I said as I looked back down into the maze of branches that the magnifinder would have fallen through to the forest floor below. Fortunately, I found it behind me wedged between the tree branch and a smaller branch growing out.

I felt it was time to go back home and get some rest before returning tonight. LaCroiux had believed that King Steven would attempt to move the emerald into the castle at night to avoid a commotion. If the word spread that an emerald had again been found in Mistasia, it would become a special event drawing everyone within the Kingdom and beyond.

I held the magnifinder securely as I began to descend. I took one last look through the open end, mostly to make sure I hadn't cracked the glass when I almost fell.

"What's that?" I said as I discovered two elves in Cadieux Village. I caught a glimpse of a green light as the sun, which had risen above the castle behind them, shown across the object in a female elf's hands. "The emerald!"

I dashed back to speak with Sorcerer LaCroiux.

"The emerald," I shouted after entering LaCroiux's chamber deep within Woverine Forest. I needed to catch my breath before continuing. "I saw the emerald in the village, Master!"

"Good." LaCroiux's head lifted, and a sharp chuckle emerged. It was startling. I had not heard him laugh very often.

The sound was full and aggressive...much like his demeanor. "You have done well, my apprentice. Are you ready for your journey?"

When I entered he was working on a new contraption. It was a small, square box. It was made from a material similar to that of the elven warriors' shields. I had caught myself staring at his work and didn't answer, which was angering him.

"Ethan!" My master shouted to regain my attention. "It is now time for you to return to your family," he stated matter-of-factly.

A sudden sinking feeling appeared in my gut. "What? I..."

He interrupted me, "This is not up for discussion." He quickly returned to working on his project as if I wasn't standing shocked in the same room.

"You want me to leave?" LaCroiux didn't respond immediately. Finally, I turned to leave.

"Ethan, your opportunity to prove that you are the strongest Whizzenmog has arisen. It is time to claim your place in Cadieux Castle beside the rightful ruler of Mistasia. You will see me again soon when we are reunited at the throne, my apprentice. First, you must steal the emerald, Ethan."

I had just assumed that when Sorcerer LaCroiux requested that I observe the daily routine of the guards around Cadieux Castle, it was for the planning of an attack against the king to find out when the king might be vulnerable. Now, I am charged with reentering the castle and stealing its most prized possession...the last emerald.

I now found myself walking away from what had become my home, The Wolverine Forest, and back to the place I had dreaded I would someday have to return...Cadieux Castle. I shuffled my paws along the grass leaving a trail behind me. My wand gripped tightly in my left paw, I glided my right paw across its smooth edge toward the tip. Never before had I felt this uneasy...this nervous. Not even the night I was carried away to LaCroiux's hideout by a Wolverine. Today, the sun hung high in the sky over Dragon Lake. It looked like a giant pancake atop the perfectly still water, which reminded me that I was hungry, but I didn't want to eat. My stomach was too upset right now to tolerate any food.

"My father won't be happy to see me," I muttered.

I reached Cadieux Village just before night fall. The moon had switched places with the sun. It aided me in my journey to the edge of the small village where most of the elves lived. These elves were extremely loyal to King **Steven**. They worked around the castle performing any jobs necessary for the kingdom, including protection, when called upon.

As I walked up the narrow pathway between the small houses I could feel eyes watching me. The farther I travelled up the path the stronger that sensation became.

I stopped. Someone was behind me. When I turned around, no one was there. I searched for figures in the darkness. I saw what looked like a slender elven warrior, but as the wind blew, I realized it was nothing more than the shadow cast by a nearby tree.

Quickly, I moved toward the castle's back gate at the edge of Cadieux Village. The front of the grey stone structure was actually on the opposite side facing the ocean.

At the door, were two elven warriors, and they weren't very happy to see me approaching.

"Stop right there, Ethan Whizzenmog!" The elf to my right barked. "You are not welcome here any longer."

"But this is my home," I coyly replied.

"Your father claims that you abandoned your home to live with the evils of the Wolverine Forest," the second elf retorted.

I growled at him and pointed my wand at his chest. "Summon my father. We will let him decide." I don't know what had come over me, but I had suddenly developed the courage of a Whizzenmog.

The elf to my right dashed into the castle and quickly returned. "You are clear to pass!"

I stared down the two elves as I walked past them in through the open door of Cadieux Castle. The familiar smell of wet stone and mildew entered my keen nostrils. I looked to the ceiling as I passed under the large opening. There between the inner and outer stone walls hung large black metal chains that controlled the gate. Many other elves glared at me as I walked past. It was more than obvious that my return was not welcomed.

"Ethan!" a familiar voice shouted. Before I could turn my head and see who called my name, a pair of reddish orange arms wrapped themselves around me and lifted me into the air.

It was my brother, Rainer Whizzenmog, who clutched me tightly and spun me around like a spinning top.

"Please, put me down, Rainer," I cried thanking the heavens that I hadn't eaten anything today.

"You have returned," Rainer stated with glee and the biggest smile I had ever seen. His eyes were wide and his ears pointed straight up. "Oh, brother, I missed you, Ethan!" He said and then hugged me once again.

I attempted to hold back my emotions, but couldn't. A sudden swell of happiness to see him came over me. It felt strangely good to once again be in Cadieux Castle, but I had yet to see my father, who would most definitely react differently.

Rainer hastily whisked me away to meet up with our father. We dashed past the tall wooden doors bearing the crest of the king, Steven Cadieux, and stopped just outside the next set of doors.

These doors were far smaller and darker in color. They were very old, but still in good condition. Rainer brashly flicked his wand and the doors opened. He waved me inside the room...a room in which my father would surely be awaiting me.

My stomach turned and I inhaled deeply. I felt my brother's paw against my back as he began to lightly push me in the right direction. He again motioned for me to walk inside. It felt like a trap. I felt like I would walk in there and the door would close behind me, then a giant troll would snatch me off the ground and bite my head off.

"Come on, Ethan," Rainer urged as he dragged me in by my arm.

The room was poorly lit. Only a few candles hung along the walls in this circular room. A small bed was at the far end. In the bed I could see the figure of my father under his covers. I had forgotten just how late it was.

"Is father asleep?" I asked Rainer, who continued to drag me across the stone floor.

"Yes. He will be so surprised to see you, Ethan!"

"Wait!" I pulled my arm back from Rainer's strong grip.

"You told them to let me into the castle?"

"So what!" my brother replied.

"Our father doesn't even know that I am here...does he?" I suddenly felt a panic setting in. This was a trap.

"Everything is just fine, Ethan. Calm down."

"Ethan?" I heard my father call in a drowsy voice. He now sat upright in bed. "Is that really you my son?"

I watched as my father reached for his wand at the side of his bed. He grasped his perfectly straight wand within his paw and turned toward me. The tip began to glow. My heart raced. Was my father about to zap me to death? His wand brightened and lit the room. My father's face instantly exploded with a smile as he dashed from his bed, tossing away the covers, and running to me. He grabbed me by the shoulders and pulled me closely. My father, a man that had never shown any affection toward me in my entire life, was hugging me.

My father walked around the castle with a smile on his face for the next few days. He didn't look like himself. I was used to a scowl or frown.

Rainer and I spent most of our time together. He was just as excited about my return. We went out to the village and sat down on two tree stumps.

"Thank you, Ethan."

"For what," I nervously laughed. **What does that mean?** I thought.

"For coming home. Father has been very upset since you left. He blamed me for you leaving."

I didn't reply. How do you reply to something like that?

"If you don't mind me asking...where exactly did you go?" Rainer wondered.

I inhaled deeply. It must have sounded like he had upset me, because Rainer quickly retracted his question.

"Just forget it. I'm just glad you came home." Rainer rubbed my back.

"It is good to be home, brother."

A few weeks later, I walked alone along the edge of Dragon Lake. It was night. Torches burned in Cadieux Village just behind me, but along the calm waterfront I could feel the chill in the air. Stars lit up the sky. I had wandered out here without realizing where I was going. This walk had begun inside the castle grounds, but I just kept going as if something was drawing me away.

A snapping sound hit my ears, like a branch breaking. It was followed by another. If someone was attempting to sneak up on me they were doing a very poor job. I searched the darkness for signs of motion, but couldn't see anyone.

"Whizzenmog!" A curt voice startled me.

I still couldn't see where it was coming from.

"Behind you, Ethan."

Standing behind me was a frightening sight. A tall slender and hideous looking creature was directly behind me. It was a vampire bat. Its wings were outstretched giving it a grand appearance.

"Who are you?" I cowardly questioned.

"It is I, Sorcerer LaCroiux," The voice sounded very familiar to that of my master, yet the figure standing before me didn't resemble him in the slightest.

"Master? How can that be?"

"I cast a spell on this dimwitted soul in order to reach you. I believe you have forgotten your task, Ethan. The emerald?"

"No…no. I haven't forgotten, master. I just am trying to gain their trust."

"Stop wasting time and get the emerald. It is everything." LaCroiux snapped through the razor-sharp teeth of the Vampire bat. Then, almost as quickly as he had appeared, he vanished by leaping skyward and flying into the darkness.

A rush of wind blew across my face signaling his departure. I searched through the sky for him, but he was gone.

Now it was apparent that Sorcerer LaCroiux was watching my every move waiting for me to steal the Last Emerald of power.

I struggled to open my eyes the next morning. My head was pounding like someone had been hitting me with a rock all throughout the night. Sitting up was difficult. My stomach felt nauseous.

The sunlight pierced through the window like a knife stabbing me in the eyes. I placed my furry forearm across my eyes to block it. This didn't help.

A rustling sound came from the far side of my room as the heavy wooden door swung open. The rusty hinges squealed. A thud echoed when the door reached the stone wall.

"Ethan? Are you okay?" Rainer asked.

I attempted to open my eyes. They burned. "No. I have a monster headache."

"Let's get you something for that," Rainer said as he now surprisingly stood next to me.

It startled me to hear his voice in a different area of the room since I couldn't see him. I felt the small tip of his wand rest against my forehead. I shrunk away.

"Hey, what are you doing?" I barked.

"Just sit still, Ethan."

I had to admit I was a bit nervous, since not that long ago I considered my brother my enemy. Well, technically he still was. A warm sensation entered my head just below my ear. It spread across my forehead. It felt like a fire had been lit between my ears, yet it didn't hurt. The warmth slowly moved down between my eyes. Tears formed and then began to stream down my checks. I could feel them moving through my fur.

"Open your eyes," Rainer said. My vision had been restored and, even more amazingly, my headache was gone.

"That's amazing."

"You're welcome, Ethan." Rainer patted my back with his strong paw. "Come on, I want to show you something."

We walked through the bustling castle, passing Elven Warriors at every turn until we reached the far end of Cadieux Castle. This was a very darkened and private area. Candles lit the hallway just enough to allow me to see a short distance.

"Where are we, Rainer?"

Rainer placed his paw over his mouth, motioning to be quiet. His usually orangish-red fur was almost black in the dimly lit hallway. He began walking and I followed. Rainer used his wand to replace the candle light as we moved farther down the hall. Rainer stopped at what appeared to be a dead end. He moved his wand attempting to find something.

"Hold this," Rainer said as he handed me his wand.

"No, like this," My brother directed. I had allowed the lighted wand to point at the floor. He showed me where to direct the light. In the lower corner, was an oddly-shaped stone.

Rainer pushed against the stone and it easily moved. The wall split and swung open.

"Hurry!" Rainer said. He grabbed my arm and pulled me inside the blackened room. I heard the stone wall close behind us, but I couldn't move. I was completely focused on the object perched on a golden pedestal in the middle of the room glimmering against the light produced from my brother's wand.

I only spent a few moments with it, but my life changed completely. I had never felt such a pure adrenaline charge like when I placed my paw on the green emerald. In an instant I knew exactly what I had to do. I would steal the emerald...not for Sorcerer LaCroiux, but for me. It would make me stronger than anyone in Mistasia. No wizard or sorcerer would stand in my way. My father would soon be bowing to a new king, but it wasn't going to be Cragon Cadieux...it would be me!

MORNING OF TRUTH

4

My mind had become overrun with thoughts of the emerald. Its beauty. Its power. Now all that remained was how I would steal it.

Rainer came to get me the following morning. I was eager to see where he would take me today...hoping it was to see the Last Emerald again. To my disappointment, he took me to the Proving Grounds just outside the castle. It was where Rainer and I used to battle while practicing our wizardry. Therefore, this was a place of bad memories for me. It was the last place I had been before running away, and since my return I had avoided it.

"Why did you bring me here Rainer?" I said with shortness in my tone.

"Father asked me to meet him here this morning. He has a very important assignment for me."

"So why am I here?"

"I hoped you would join me," He said it with such heartfelt sincerity I almost believed him.

I scoffed. My brother's reaction showed that he actually meant it. I suddenly felt uncomfortable.

"You really want me with you?" I asked.

Rainer smiled and nodded.

I smiled back but didn't respond. Rainer had been trying very hard to repair our friendship since I returned, but I continued to keep my distance. It would only make what would happen easier for us all.

"Rainer, are you ready?" Our father's voice joyously rang out into the Proving Grounds. He hesitated upon noticing me standing next to Rainer. "Ethan, good morning, son. I didn't know you were going to be here." The surprise in his voice seeped forth like the smoke from an uncontrolled flame. It hung over my head casting a dark shadow. This was the father I'd expected upon my return to the castle. Loveless and ashamed.

"I asked him to join me father," My brother replied.

Our father's eyes moved sharply between us as though he was attempting to figure out if I had some sort of spell cast over Rainer. Surely, my brother couldn't be acting of right mind to invite me. After a moment, he cleared his throat in what appeared to be an attempt at ridding himself of whatever he actually wanted to say, but he thought better of it. Then proceeded to address Rainer and ignore me.

"Rainer, the king and queen will be making a journey to the northern territory of Mistasia and I need you to join them as their protector."

My brother's face was overjoyed. It was a great honor to be the keeper of the royal family's protection.

"I must remain here at the castle." My father suddenly stopped his explanation. He was unaware that I knew about the last emerald being here and that Rainer had shown me its location. It was obviously the reason he wasn't joining the King and Queen on their trip. He was always at their side.

"I'm trusting you with their safety."

"Thank you, Father." Rainer bowed his head.

Our father glanced in my direction for a moment. The emotion he had shown me the night I had returned was nowhere to be recognized. Then he turned and left.

Rainer was excited. "This is amazing. Brother, you must promise to come with me. It would mean a great deal to have you by my side."

"I don't think that is such a good idea, Rainer." I was referring to both the fact that our father obviously didn't want me to go and the fact that I would be away from the castle, which made it more difficult to steal the emerald.

He placed his strong paw on my shoulder and looked me in the eyes. He looked down upon me, standing a full head taller.

"Please, Ethan. It would be good for us to spend time together. I have missed you so much, brother." Then he pulled me close and hugged me so tightly it became hard to breathe.

I agreed to go with him but quickly regretted my decision.

"Great. We leave tonight!"

Rainer dashed off to collect supplies and weaponry for the journey. I stood stuck in the grass...not literally, but just unable to move my feet. I hoped that if I didn't reenter the castle I wouldn't have to go tonight. It also meant that I would have to wait until my return to steal the emerald.

The air had cooled since Rainer and I were in the Proving Grounds earlier in the day. The wind had picked up. It blew through my fur and cut into my skin like a thousand tiny arrows. Fires from the village where doused. I watched as a few elves scrambled to relight them, but the winds made it a worthless attempt. Most gave up and returned to their homes.

I stood alone in the field between Cadieux Castle and the village. Closing my eyes I could see the glowing green emerald hidden away within the castle.

"Ethan," A voice whispered in my ears. I opened my eyes, but no one was around. My gaze fixed in the distance...the exact place where I knew Sorcerer LaCroiux's hideout was deep within the Wolverine Forest. The tree tops were barely visible beyond Dragon Lake. Again I closed my eyes, when I heard my name repeated whistling in the winds. My master was calling to me.

Then, something landed on my shoulder. I jumped and brandished my wand.

"Ethan, it's me!" Rainer yelled.

"I'm sorry, Rainer. You just startled me."

Rainer smiled at me. He was so excited about our journey. I on the other hand, was dreading the next few days. We walked through the village making small talk, but discussing nothing important. I found myself drifting in and out of the conversation until we stood before a large pile of wood sitting next to the lake.

I didn't say anything right away, just looked at my brother waiting for the explanation, because his expression showed that he was not surprised to see the enormous pile of trees cut and laying on their sides in a triangular stack.

"I had the elves gather wood for us."

"Really? Do we have enough?" I sarcastically asked while looking into the sky to see the top of the pile.

Rainer chuckled slightly and slapped me in the chest lightheartedly. "Come on, Ethan."

"Are we building a fort?" I asked.

"Ah...no. We are building a boat for the king and queen to use on their journey up Red River tonight." He said this as though it was a small feat. Just create a ship that by the look of the wood pile would be able to transport every elf living in the kingdom.

"Well, you have fun with that." I replied jokingly.

Rainer held his wand out and began motioning the wood to move. In just a short time, Rainer had moved most of the wood into smaller piles and had begun molding and shaping them like pieces of clay.

"Are you just going to stand there?" Rainer questioned while flattening one tree trunk into a plank board that he used to create a small section of the ship's deck.

I scoffed and shook my head in disbelief that I found myself building a boat for two people that I planned to remove from the throne.

It only took the two of us a little over two hours, but by the time the royal family began to gather with their assembly at the edge of Cadieux Village, we placed the finishing touches on a magnificent vessel worthy of carrying the king and queen along

Red River. The boat was tall and narrow with sails made from woven tree leaves and cattails from around the lake.

We quickly set sail.

The air remained cool as the sun completed its journey over the edge of the world. Stars slowly began to emerge one by one like creatures peeking out from their homes and looking to see if it was safe to venture out and play with one another. A calm settled into my body like I had never felt before. The smell of the salty water rushed below us and mixed with fragrances from the Wolverine Forest.

"Ethan," A voice whispered.

My heart quickened its pace, energizing my body. A surge of adrenaline burst through my veins to my paws. It was the unmistakable voice of my master calling to me from the Wolverine Forest which was laid out before us.

"Be prepared," his voice commanded.

"Ethan," Rainer's voice rang out clearly breaking LaCroiux's hold over me.

"Yes," I responded while attempting to swallow my fear.

"Are you okay?"

I nodded, but could tell that it really hadn't satisfied Rainer's worry.

"Is there something wrong? Do you sense something?"

"No. That is ridiculous," I awkwardly laughed at the thought hoping he didn't really know the truth and was just waiting for me to admit it. I was becoming paranoid. "Do you?"

"No, my brother, I wasn't gifted with such senses." Rainer replied.

It couldn't have been more than a few seconds after he finished when I heard it for the first time in my life. It was a sound that I would never forget. The dreadful screeching of Sorcerer LaCroiux's new pets...Vampire bats. The soulless creatures from the Deadly Spray Forest descended upon our ship with wings spread, claws drawn and fangs exposed. Even in the moonlight they were mightily frightening.

Two crashed down on the deck. Their wings spanned over both sides of the ship. They were much taller than our Elven Warriors, and so quick.

I drew my wand, as did my brother. We each blasted a Vampire bat. Rainer's spell landed directly on his target's chest flinging the retched beast from the ship and into Red River. My shot was not so precise. It hit the vampire bat's left wing, which caused the beast to screech at us. The high-pitched wail stabbed my ears like a million knives. I covered them with my paws, but it gave little relief. Rainer fired again sending the other vampire bat off the ship and into the dark waters below.

43

There were dozens more buzzing above us like pesky bugs. We ducked when one swooped in and sliced at us with its razor-sharp claws. The deck of the ship was in chaos as the Elven Warriors battled the Vampire bats. Some used bow and arrow, picking off the bats as they dove in for a chance to knock an elf into the waters below. I watched as a young elf met just that fate and tumbled over the rail into the darkness.

"Watch out!" Rainer barked as another winged creature dove toward us.

I raised my wand, but found myself frozen, unable to cast a spell to save myself. The creature closed in fast, but my brother tackled me just as its claws missed my furry face.

"What are you doing?" I asked slightly annoyed.

"Saving your life!" Rainer quickly stood up and began searching for something in the chaos of our ship.

"What are you looking for, Rainer?"

"The King and Queen!" he replied.

A bright flash of light exploded at the far end of the ship, which was now rocking violently back and forth.

"What was that?" Rainer asked. He ran off before I could venture a guess, but I was pretty certain that I knew what had just happened.

I followed my brother as he moved through the battle like a maze, ducking and dodging arrows and swords. A Vampire bat jumped in front of him, but Rainer blasted the beast out of the way without hesitating. It was actually pretty impressive to see his courage.

When we reached the far end of the ship where we had seen the light, I caught my first glimpse of our plot taking form. Sorcerer LaCroiux held the queen around the neck as the king pleaded for her release. LaCroiux wore a long gray robe with a hood to guard his face, but I could feel his presence.

"Release her!" Rainer demanded. He held his wand at the ready. After standing there looking back and forth between LaCroiux and Rainer for a moment attempting to figure out who I should be pointing my wand at I chose Rainer...and then quickly swung it over to LaCroiux before my brother noticed.

Am I supposed to reveal I'm a bad guy yet? I thought.

"Let her go, now!" my brother barked. He looked so calm and courageous. I found myself proud of him just when I should have wished for Rainer to crumble under the pressure.

I could barely see the glimmer in my master's eye hidden in the shadow of his hood, but it was there. Everything was going according to his plan, and now it was time for his next move.

LaCroiux released the queen, who rushed back into King Steven's awaiting arms. Just as he grabbed her and pulled her close LaCroiux struck.

"Portio!" He yelled. A bright orange light escaped his hand. It moved through the air like it was riding a wave into shore before reaching the king and queen and engulfing them. It grew brighter by the second until it hurt my eyes to watch.

I closed my eyes and turned away. When the brightness diminished they were gone. The only thing remaining was the wicked yellow smile of Sorcerer Pierre LaCroiux, which gleamed from his shadowy face.

"NO!" Rainer cried. His panicked voice sent a chill up my spine. He reacted so quickly, firing spell after spell in a dazzling array of light directly at my master.

LaCroiux calmly deflected each spell seemingly sorting them by color into certain directions. Then, when he seemed to have grown tired of this sad attempt at an attack, he mustered up a fireball and hurled it into Rainer's chest. My brother collapsed.

"Rainer," I ran to his aid. He was breathing, but was unconscious and very warm to the touch, yet not burned. "What are you doing?" I angrily questioned my master.

"Ending this," LaCroiux removed his hood. His long braided beard emerged first against the moonlight. He walked toward my wounded brother like an animal stalks its prey. There was a glint of red in his eyes.

"No," I began to say when LaCroiux grabbed me by the neck and lifted me up. My paws dangled in the air, and I couldn't breathe.

"Retrieve the stone, Ethan." Then, he flung me down on top of Rainer. Another flash of orange light burned my eyes and then it was completely dark.

BATTLE OF BROTHERS

<u>5</u>

"Ethan!" My brother called "Ethan, get up!

I knew when I opened my eyes I would no longer be on the ship, just like the king and queen vanished. Sorcerer LaCroiux had transported them somewhere using his powers. I also had a pretty good idea where Rainer and I ended up...Cadieux Castle. "Retrieve the stone, Ethan," LaCroiux's words echoed in my head. He would have to send us back to the castle for me to retrieve the last emerald of power. I was alarmed at what I saw outside the castle when I opened my eyes...a battle!

"Get up, NOW!" Rainer yelled as he pulled me up off the ground.

My eyes were definitely wide open. The castle was under attack. Sorcerer LaCroiux had given me assistance in the form of hundreds of wolverines and a few large trolls. The Elven Warriors valiantly defended the castle, as did our father. He was directly in the middle of the battlefield fending off two or three wolverines at a time.

"We have to help father!" Rainer said as he continued to pull me toward the action.

I personally didn't want any part of this battle. I wanted to find a way through it and into the castle. Searching through the groups of Elven Warriors and wolverines, I found a path to the back gate. Rainer stopped me.

"Where are you going?"

Do I zap him or play along? I wondered. Then I remembered that I would need his help to enter the room where the emerald was hidden so I played along. I picked the first wolverine I saw and blasted him in the back.

"Great shot, Ethan!" my brother cheered.

A smile crept across my face. I blasted two more. It felt good. **Don't shoot the elves.** I reminded myself. Besides they would be my servants soon.

I suddenly realized that my father, brother and I had formed a triangle defense so no enemy could sneak up behind us. We were easily fending off LaCroiux's mighty henchmen.

"Rainer! Ethan!" our father called. "I need you both to get to the castle."

I immediately began searching for the safest route.

"I can help, father!" Rainer replied.

"I need you two protecting the princess."

That seemed to be all Rainer needed to hear, and we were off toward the castle. Once we reached the back gate we slipped inside and quickly found the princess. The castle shook as the monstrous trolls hammered away on the walls with their meaty fists trying to punch a hole through the stones. Fortunately, this castle was well built and would keep them at bay long enough for me to steal the emerald and end this insanity.

The young princess was crying when we arrived, and her uncle Cragon Cadieux was in the room. I gasped at the sight of him.

"Thank goodness you have arrived. I fear for the princess's safety," The strong, young elven prince claimed.

"Yeah, sure," I muttered, but no one seemed to hear me.

"Why are you not with my brother?" The prince questioned.

Like you don't know, I sarcastically thought. The prince sure seemed to be laying this act on thick. He knows exactly what happened on the boat, and outside the castle. He's behind it all. But, he doesn't know how I'm going to ruin his well thought out plans.

The castle shook violently again and again. With each thunderous boom, the princess cried out. A young elven girl named, Grace Tallon, held her against her chest attempting to sooth, Princess Merran Cadieux...who was now the rightful heir to the throne.

"Rainer Whizzenmog, how will your father stop this attack?"

Rainer ignored Prince Cragon. He appeared to be in deep thought, maybe trying to figure out his next move. I could almost feel his torment while he helplessly waited in the castle for the battle to end outside.

"We are losing the battle!"

"NO!" Rainer screamed. He was panting heavily trying to control his rage. I had never seen him like this before. He appeared torn.

"We have a secret weapon that could change our fortune, Rainer."

I immediately knew exactly what the prince was referring to...the last emerald.

"It is truly our only hope," Prince Cragon pleaded.

Rainer snapped his head at the prince and looked him up and down struggling to maintain eye contact. My brother was fighting within himself whether to open the hidden chamber and release the power within the emerald to save the castle, or hope that our father could stop the onslaught before it was too late.

That is when I decided to enter the fray with the good prince...for now. I calmly placed my hand upon my brother's shoulder. "Rainer, you have already failed father once tonight." I said reminding him that Sorcerer LaCroiux had kidnapped the king and queen under his guard. "Don't do it again."

A tear formed in Rainer's eye. "Let's go!" He gave in.

I instructed Grace to lock the door from the inside and hide until we returned. Something I had no intention of doing. Prince Cragon and I followed Rainer as he ran through the castle to the secluded wing where the emerald was hidden. He opened the secret doorway and we entered. I reached for the glowing green gemstone, but it magically lifted into the air and over my head. When I turned around, it was firmly in the grasp of my brother's paw. He sternly glared at me. Prince Cragon's face lit up with excitement at the very sight of the emerald.

"It's astonishing," Prince Cragon commented. A reflection off the emerald shown in his eyes.

I caught myself staring. It had grown uncomfortable in the small room, when the prince reached out for the emerald. I don't think he realized he was doing it. The gemstone was drawing him to it. Rainer pulled it away. I saw an opportunity and snatched it from his grasp. We all began to struggle attempting to pry the emerald from one another's grip. I freed it, when Prince Cragon punched me square in the snout. My eyes instantly began to tear, and I dropped the emerald. My brother snagged it using his wand and was off running. I zapped the prince with a freezing spell for socking me, and followed Rainer into the hallway.

As I turned the corner, a flash of light blinded me. Then I saw my master. He stood across from me with Rainer between us trapping him. By now, he had probably figured out that I was not playing on his team anymore, but if he wasn't certain, I was going to make it crystal clear.

"Give it to me, brother." I demanded.

Rainer responded by pointing his wand at me. He began to back into the wall feeling LaCroiux's presence creeping up behind him. We converged on my brother. Rainer frantically swung his wand between us, pointing it at me, then LaCroiux and back again.

I reached out for the emerald and Rainer swatted at me. When our paws collided I felt a warm sensation again as the orange light reappeared. This time I heard a loud snap and everything again went black.

When we reappeared, I again found myself in a familiar place, but I knew that Rainer would not recognize our location. We were deep within the Wolverine Forest...my new home.

It was eerily quiet within the forest, as it should be since most of its inhabitants were currently at the castle. A calming sensation settled into my previously rigid body. I felt my paws relax and conform to the dirty forest floor. Inhaling deeply, the aroma of the forest zoomed through me. An evil smile overtook my face. One I couldn't resist even if I tried. I now realized that only my brother stood between me and the emerald. Sorcerer LaCroiux made certain of that by sending us here alone.

"Rainer? Where are you, my brother?"

I listened to the forest talking to me. Birds chirped, leaves rustled against the slight breeze. Then, a sound. Something produced only by another stepping on a twig. I spun around. My wand at the ready

"I don't want to hurt you, Rainer. I only want the emerald."

A rustling sound rose from my left. "Never!" Rainer yelled as he ran toward me. He leaped and crashed into me, knocking my wand into a pile of leaves. We rolled along the forest floor throwing punches, which is an odd way for two wizards to settle anything, but our brotherly spat went much deeper than just this emerald. I grabbed hold of Rainer's fur and flung him against an exposed root. He yelled out in pain as I pinned him down.

"Where is the emerald?"

We were both breathing heavily. He struggled to free himself. "I have hidden it in the woods. You'll never find it."

Angered, I slammed his head against the ground. The ground trembled as my powers began to boil. As a wizard, I needed my wand to channel my powers into use, but as a sorcerer I was free to twist the elements around me.

I began to laugh. It was unexplainable. There was no good reason for laughter at this moment, but I couldn't control it. Fear had taken over Rainer's face. He had begun to realize just how much danger he was in.

"How could you do this, Ethan? How could you betray your own family?"

"My family?" My laughter ceased and was replaced with rage. The swell of emotions caused me to tear down a nearby tree. It crashed to the ground only a few feet behind me. "You ask me how I could betray my family? This family? I was never a part of the Whizzenmog family, Rainer. Our father never accepted me for what I wasn't."

"And what's that?"

I hesitated briefly deciding whether or not to answer truthfully, then I did, "You, Rainer. I was never as good and strong as you." I summoned more roots from the ground. They burst out tossing dirt into the air, which landed on Rainer's face and body covering his reddish-orange fur. I directed the roots to entangle his body and hold him to the ground.

"I will find the emerald, Rainer."

"Why are you so angry?" Rainer questioned.

I scoffed at the thought that he was unaware of the reason. "Do you remember the night I left? What you did to me? Humiliating me again! The look in our father's eyes that night said it all. I knew that I would never be as good as you in his eyes. That was the day he choose you, Rainer."

"That's not true."

"LIAR!" I screamed so loudly that the chirping birds leapt into the sky and flew away. "Liar," I repeated in a whisper.

"He was crushed when you didn't return, Ethan."

"Well...father won't have to worry now, because when I find that emerald, I am going to be the most powerful sorcerer in Mistasia. And you will call me King."

Rainer didn't respond. He just stared at me shocked, like I had just slapped him in the face.

"Now where did you hide the emerald, Rainer," I asked while searching around the forest.

When I turned my back, a bright blue flash caught my eye, followed by a snapping. I turned to see Rainer had broken free and escaped into the forest. I followed him forgetting about my wand in the leaves. It didn't matter. I had left that life behind now. I was a sorcerer and in this forest there were all the weapons I would ever need to defeat my brother.

First, I pulled the ground up under his feet causing him to trip. Rainer gathered himself and ran again. Next, I snapped a nearby limb free and flung it like an arrow. My brother blocked it with a charm and continued to flee. He hid behind a large tree, but I just yanked it from the ground, roots and all, before tossing it aside with a tremendous crash which crippled at least two more trees nearby.

Rainer attempted to slow me down with a freezing spell, but I pulled the dirt before me up like a shield. It froze, but I kicked my leg through and continued stalking him.

"Give me the emerald, Rainer!" I demanded.

Rainer started to run again, but I had had enough. A tree branch lodged into the ground blocking his path. He turned to the right and another landed in front of him; then two more encircled Rainer in a wooden prison.

"There's no escaping this forest, Rainer!" I stuck my face between two branches. "For so long, I envied you. Now, I pity you. I will not ask you again."

Rainer pointed to a bush located between two trees just a short distance away. Underneath, I could see a green glow. My heart began to quicken as I reached underneath and grabbed hold of the solid stone. I pulled it out and focused on the object in my hand. It was green in color, but was not the emerald…just a mere rock.

"Rainer!" I yelled in frustration, but when I turned around he was gone again. He had escaped from my trap and disappeared into the forest. I closed my eyes and knelt to the ground. Placing my paw along the forest floor I calmed myself. I could feel the vibrations flowing to me from my right side. I dashed off in pursuit.

The forest quickly thinned and I found myself at its edge. Before me was a clearing. In the distance, Rainer ran for the shelter of a small house. I dashed toward him running faster than I had ever gone in my life. Just before I reached him, Rainer gripped the emerald tightly in his hands and was chanting something.

I didn't have the time to reach him, when the ground began to tremble. I skidded to a halt. That was when I noticed our family's crest upon the large wooden door. This was our old family home from centuries ago, before we became the protectors to the king. The land had claimed most of the house; only this door remained visible under the green vines, and tall grass.

The emerald began to glow brightly in Rainer's palms. The wooden door began to change. It started to swirl around and around. Flashes of light spun at great speed. Rainer glanced at me for a single moment and then jumped into the portal. He had vanished.

I had to follow. I ran the short remaining distance and jumped, crashing into the decaying wooden door. I burst through into the dark and dirty room behind. The portal was gone, Rainer was gone, and most importantly...the emerald was gone with him.

I was crushed. My hope for greatness had just vanished before my eyes. I pulled myself out of the wreckage and stepped out into the grass. Standing at the edge of the forest was my master, Sorcerer LaCroiux. Fear overtook me.

PUNISHMENT

6

Sorcerer LaCroiux's eyes were fixated upon me. **How much had he seen? Did he know that my brother had escaped? Did he know Rainer had the emerald?** All these thoughts raced through my mind. My head was swimming, my stomach flipped with fear. I quickly got my answer.

The elder elven sorcerer lashed out. He lifted me into the air. I floated above the ground as the wind carried me toward my master. LaCroiux briskly guided me to the edge of the forest and then released his grip on me. I crashed, landing hard on my side. My elbow lodged into my ribs knocking the wind from my lungs. I gasped for air as LaCroiux picked me up by my neck with his bony fingers sticking into my fur. He still hadn't spoken to me.

Our eyes meet for a brief moment. It frightened me to see into his devilish soul from such a close distance. I struggled to speak causing LaCroiux's head to tilt in an odd fashion. A smug grin invaded his old slightly wrinkled skin.

"Speak up, Ethan." Then he released his grip and I fell back to the ground. "Where is the emerald you ignorant fool?"

"It is gone." I braced for an attack, but he didn't strike.

"Gone?"

"My brother stole it from me and then vanished into some kind of spinning portal. I chased after him, but it disappeared before I could follow."

Sorcerer LaCroiux stared at the broken door in the distance where he must have witnessed my brother's disappearance.

"You have failed me, Ethan. You're father was right. You are a disappointment."

My body trembled. I couldn't bring myself to look at my master. All the strength and power I had felt just a few short moments ago was now gone. I was left cowering like a small child.

"You will have to pay for your failure, Ethan." The powerful sorcerer didn't hesitate.

He tossed a bright blue fireball at me. It engulfed me. At first it actually felt cool around my body, but at the snap of his fingers the color changed to a scorching white and the intense heat ripped through my body. I could smell my skin burning. The pain was excruciating. I screamed for him to stop, but he continued. My fur began to burst into flames and crumble from my body. The skin underneath was covered in heat blisters, which began to burst and then boil under the tremendous heat

61

directly on my skin. Sorcerer LaCroiux was cooking me alive. My skin began to peel and stretch revealing a scaly layer underneath. I couldn't take much more. I wished for death, but then the pain stopped. My vision began to blur and fade to black. I collapsed to the ground and passed out.

When I awoke, we were no longer in Wolverine Forest. LaCroiux had taken us back to Cadieux Castle. He had let me live. I found myself on the stone cold floor of my father's bedroom. I was alone. I struggled to my feet and stumbled into a wooden chair, barely catching myself before I fell to the floor. I pulled myself along the wall to the bed. My chest felt tight and my side hurt. I began to cry when I saw the skin on my arms. There was no longer any fur. It was completely gone. My skin was scaly and had a brownish-yellow color, like I was sickly. I lifted my head slowly almost too afraid to glance in the mirror and see my reflection. I gasped aloud at the sight of myself.

"NO!" I screamed. I now resembled some hideously deformed creature, a cross between a snake and an elf. My eyes were deep red and bulging from the sides of my head, with two large fangs and a forked tongue.

LaCroiux had exacted his punishment for me losing the emerald of power. I would forever remember my failure.

I sat alone in my father's room. The sun had risen and begun to set again, when the door creaked open and three elven warriors entered with swords drawn. They stepped to the side as Sorcerer LaCroiux swooped in with a gleeful smile and joyous tone in his voice as though he had never been mad at me.

"Ethan! You are going to miss the celebration!" His demeanor was a far cry from our last encounter. His appearance had changed drastically too, as he now wore royal robes; a long white robe with gold and purple designs along one side and a metal staff with an empty place in the top which looked like it was made to hold something specific. "Come Ethan, we are requested at this celebration!"

I followed LaCroiux to the upper most part of the castle that overlooked the village. Gathered below was the entire population of Cadieux. I stood quietly beside my master as we waited patiently, but I dared not ask why. I was afraid to even look in his direction, so I just stared at the ground allowing me to notice that even my feet had changed. They now looked like lizard claws of the same color as my skin. One tear streamed down my scaly cheek.

Music began to blare. The crowd began to make noise, some cheered, some gasped and other cried as I did.

Then Cragon Cadieux walked from the opening out onto the balcony joining LaCroiux and me. He was wearing the king's robes. Long, thick black material with the royal colors woven in all around the edges...purple and gold just like LaCroiux's. Cragon wore a smile that beamed from ear to ear. He had won. The plot against his own brother had materialized almost exactly the way he and my master had planned...except for the emerald, for which I paid dearly.

Grace Tallon emerged behind Cragon. She looked distraught as she carried the young elven princess in her arms. Her uncle turned and removed Princess Merran from her care giver's unwilling release. Grace was quickly pulled back and escorted away. The crowd erupted in a chaotic array of yelling, with some cheering mixed in. Then the moment every inhabitant of Mistasia would regret took place. Sorcerer LaCroiux carefully placed the crown of King Steven on the top of his brother's head. At that instant, King Cragon Cadieux emerged victorious before all of Mistasia.

REDEMPTION

7

It was extremely difficult for me to live in Cadieux Castle for many years after my father's death at the hands of my master's Wolverine Army. I knew I was mostly responsible for his demise. I was forced to spend my nights in my father's old room. I slept very little, and when I would drift off, I'd awake from terrible nightmares. In each terrifying dream I was the one that killed my father, even though I wasn't sure how he had died. I never saw him after Rainer and I left him in the fields between Cadieux Village and the castle. The lack of sleep made me uncomfortable in my tight, dry skin. It itched all the time. Some nights I wouldn't even make it to the dreams about my father because my skin would burn so badly, just as it did the day LaCroiux turned me into this...this thing.

Rainer never returned. Sometimes I would sneak away and watch from the edge of the forest with the magnifinder LaCroiux made hoping to see my brother return...with the emerald in hand.

I spent my existence in servitude to my master and the king.

Recently, LaCroiux returned to the castle in a flash as he did on most occasions, but this time with a vibrant smile. He called to me immediately. He pulled me inside the castle and into a secluded room in a far wing.

"Do you recognize this room, Ethan?"

I searched the small darkened room for any clue as to where we were. Then suddenly, an image of the emerald glowing brightly in the center of the room emerged in my mind.

"The emerald!"

"Yes," LaCroiux acknowledged my wide-eyed recognition. "I have located your brother, Ethan. Here is your opportunity to redeem yourself."

"Yes, I'll do anything, master?"

"I have discovered a way to reopen the portal that your brother created using the emerald of power so many years ago. Now, you will go through the portal and lure him here," LaCroiux said as he grabbed me by the arm and led me back into the hallway.

An orange flash of light meant we were travelling. Now we were in the Wolverine Forest.

"Aren't I to steal the emerald?" I asked

"I doubt very much that Rainer will carelessly leave it laying about for you to steal, so we need to make him want to return...and return with the emerald."

"What must I do?"

"You will go through the portal and steal something from him. His family."

"What?" I responded.

"His grand child, a girl. You will kidnap her, Ethan, and bring here to Mistasia."

LaCroiux explained how I would need to enter the portal, travel through the woods and then enter a house just beyond. Inside would be a young girl. He handed me a white pouch, within it was a powder that would reopen the portal allowing me to return to Mistasia with the girl.

He grabbed a handful of the powder from the pouch and tossed it at my feet. The ground began to shake and tremble. Then it started to spin and swirl. I had seen this once before, when my brother disappeared forever. **Was LaCroiux tricking me? Was he punishing me one last time? Would the ground open up and I be sucked down into the depths never to be seen again?**

I would soon find out. I felt a tugging on my feet, and I began to sink into the portal. LaCroiux smiled.

Just as I began to feel the portal pulling me in, Sorcerer LaCroiux hit me with a blast of ferocious wind and knocked me to the ground.

"We have company," he pointed to two Elven Warriors tracking through the forest. "Despose of them. Then use the powder to reopen another portal." He pointed to the portal as it closed. Sorcerer LaCroiux vanished in a flash with a single tap of his staff upon the ground.

I tracked through Wolverine Forest. I stopped and inhaled deeply. The scent of elves was unmistakable upon the air, sweet and fruity as it entered my reptilian nostrils. They were easy to find.

I slithered up behind them; Grace Tallon, guardian to Princess Merran Cadieux, and Mecca Begron, an elven warrior.

"Just two elves? I am hurt to know your princess thinks so little of me that she believes it takes only two Elven warriors to defeat me." I mocked.

Grace spun aiming her meager arrow directly at me. I felt laughter begin within my tainted heart. She truly believed she could stop me with a single arrow? It would take hundreds. I faked a panic and placed my hands in the air.

"I surrender."

"Really?" Mecca blurted out in astonishment.

"No," I replied with a laugh, confusing the simple-minded elf.

Grace's temper flared. She fired her arrow, but I summoned a burst of wind with a wave of my hand directing the arrow toward Mecca.

The muscular elven warrior wore armor, yet jumped out of the way just in time. It pierced the ground where he had been. Mecca brandished his sword and slashed at me.

I danced away from each attempt while laughing. **These two were the best warriors the princess could send to stop me? What a joke.** I had a task to perform. This battle was becoming bothersome. I gritted my teeth and blasted Mecca with a gust of wind knocking him to the ground. Then, I summoned tree roots around the fallen warrior. Roots burst free from the soil wrapping themselves around Mecca, trapping him.

"Grace, run!" Mecca shouted as he struggled to free himself.

I spun toward Grace. She ran.

For a moment, I wondered if I should chase.

"Dispose of them!" my master's voice echoed in my head.

I chased the fleet-footed warrior through the forest. Grace ducked under roots and between the trees. Her sweet scent led me directly to her. I discovered her hiding behind a group of intertwined tree trucks.

"Tell me, Grace Tallon." I whispered in her ear after slinking up beside her unnoticed.

She turned to face me and raised her bow and arrow.

"How do you think you're going to stop me? Do you really believe you alone can defeat me? I've already defeated your weak friend."

"Just give me one good shot, Whizzenmog. That's all I need." Grace defiantly replied.

We glared at each other. I stalled her as my next attack approached. A rhythmic rustling emerged in the distance. A wicked smirk overcame my scaly face. A new scent reached my nostrils. Wolverines. Their strong, pungent odor was distinctive and overpowering in small numbers. This approaching scent was nearly deadly to those not accustom to it.

"This is my cue to leave, my dear. Tell the princess I'll take care of everything. It was good to see you...for the last time."

I moved with great haste back toward the Whizzenmog dwelling just outside Wolverine Forest.

There would be the perfect place to reopen the portal. My large reptilian feet stood firmly in the short wet grass at the edge of the forest. The sun was setting with a pink glow changing the color of the sky around it to light purple.

I closed my eyes to compose myself for a moment. The excitement of my redemption was overwhelming. My heart pulsed at great speed, racing my blood through my body.

A sudden rush stabbed the air behind me. I turned just in time to block an arrow that would have struck me in the back.

"Tallon!," I hissed.

The two elven warriors had somehow survived and raced toward me.

"Don't move, Whizzenmog!" Grace barked. "It's over!"

"Over?" I questioned the crazy thoughts of a diluted warrior. "You are too weak to defeat me?"

"I am far from weak, Whizzenmog. You are weak. Your whole family was nothing but thieves and betrayers," The angered elf scolded.

"My family betrayed me!" I screamed in pain. "It was my brother who turned out to be weak."

"I heard you helped him steal the last emerald," Grace replied arrow now pointed at my chest.

"No, but I will retrieve it from him." I removed the small pouch given to me by LaCroiux and poured a sand-like powder into my palm. I leapt back into the air and tossed the powder on the wooden door of the old Whizzenmog home.

A bright light flashed followed by rushing winds.

The elven warriors struggled in the tall grass.

The wooden door had changed. It was now a spinning vortex of colors. The colors slowly faded as did the powerful wind. When the colors had completely faded, all that was left in the doorway was a spinning black portal that resembled the nighttime sky.

Mecca stood up in the grass and yelled, "Grace, stop him! He's entering the portal to Greenville!"

I leapt into the portal, but Grace Tallon latched onto me as I entered the spinning black hole. We entered together and spun violently. She released her grip on me inside. The dizziness forced my eyes to shut.

When I reopened my eyes, I was alone. Grace wasn't near me. The forest was enormously tall. The blades of grass blocked my vision. I lifted my head. **That's better**, I thought. I was very low to the ground. It was quite disorienting. The trees were so tall here. I tried to move my legs, but felt my hips slide to the side. I looked back and noticed I had no legs, but my scaly body stretched out into the grass and disappeared. I lifted my hind end and there was a tail, with the white pouch at the very end. I shook with fear and heard an odd sound. I did it again and the sound returned. It was coming from me. My tail was rattling. I realized I had transformed into a snake.

I panicked. I needed to return to Mistasia as quickly as possible. I slithered through the grass. It wasn't very long until I reached the edge of this forest. Here it was open and raining. The grass was now shorter. In the distance was an elven-like figure sitting. She was holding a unique object above her head deflecting the water away from her body. Behind her was a home, quite a bit larger than the ones the elves called home in Mistasia.

A voice called out to her. She didn't respond. I couldn't understand what they were saying, because the rain was running down my head and across my back. I could smell the fresh water along my nostrils. I lapped at it with my forked tongue.

This was the girl that I was to retrieve. This was Rainer's grandchild. The one I must steal. It was my redemption. She stood up and walked toward the opening in the side of the home. I began to thrash my tail back and forth propelling myself across the slick grass. I was gaining on her. She entered the home and disappeared into the darkness. I slid off the grass and scratched my underbelly along a stiff rocky substance just before the door. I heard more voices calling out, but I ignored them. I was completely focused on her. I could see the funny-looking object still above her head, but her body was hidden behind a dark material. I now found myself gliding across a new substance. It was like grass, but darker and itchy. I lifted my head again as I move around to see the young girl sitting and crying.

Here was my opportunity, my redemption. I just needed to wrap myself around her and she would be mine! I sprung forward. My fangs exposed and tongue lashing. She screamed.

Sweat Redemption.

THE STORY CONTINUES IN

LAND OF MISTASIA

THE PHILLIP & WHIZZY TRILOGY (BOOK 1)

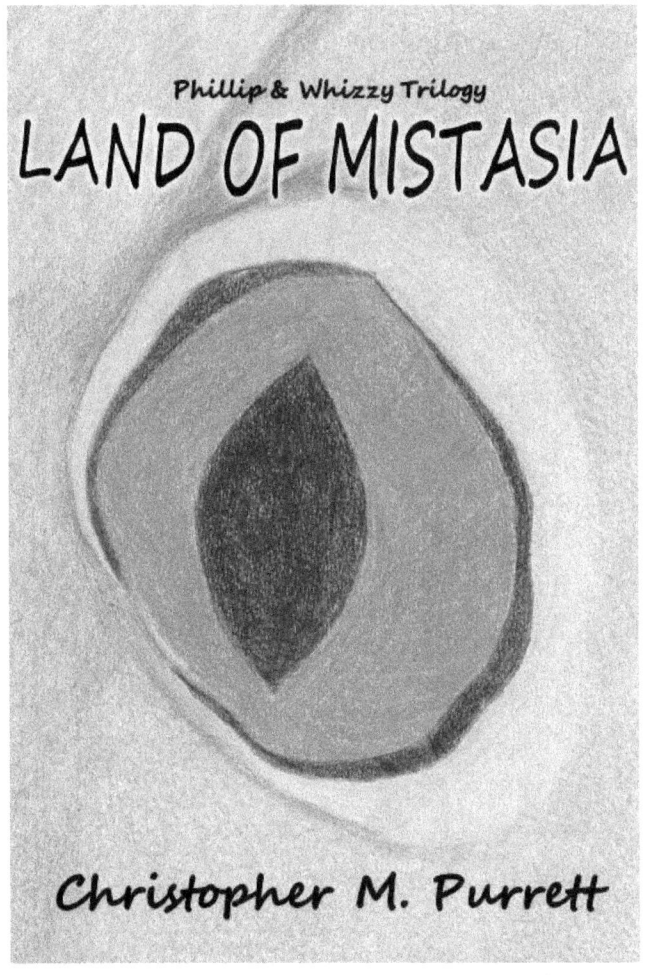

www.LandOfMistasia.com

PHILLIP & WHIZZY
TRILOGY

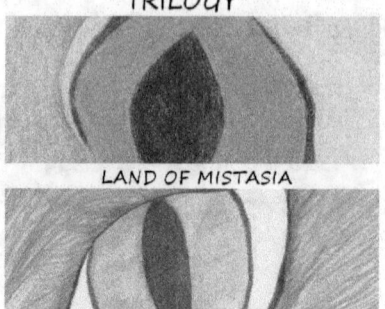

LAND OF MISTASIA

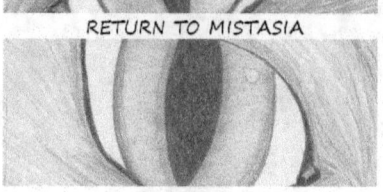

RETURN TO MISTASIA

LAST EMERALD

Available Formats

Paperback & Kindle™

Nook™

Smashwords

Keyword: Mistasia

DEAR READER!

Grace's Quest is the second novella in the Land of Mistasia storyline. It takes place between the events from Land of Mistasia (book 1) and Return to Mistasia (book 2). It is a story told by Grace Tallon about her life during the time period leading to Phillip, Whizzy and Rachel's return to Mistasia.

In this story; Queen Merran Cadieux believes that her parents are still alive, trapped in the evil Deadly Spray Forest. She sends her Elven Warrior, Grace Tallon, on a quest to save them and bring them home.

Grace travels to the Elven village known as the Outer Realm. There she discovers that Mistasia is once again turning dangerous and a familiar foe has returned to end her quest and reclaim the throne of Cadieux Castle.

I hope you enjoy this novella

Sincerely,

Christopher M. Purrett (Author)

Phillip & Whizzy Short

GRACE'S QUEST

Christopher M. Purrett

www.LandofMistasia.com

www.Purrett.com

CHAPTERS

GRACE TALLON

1

I felt the sharp edges of bark against my sensitive-skinned talons as I perched high in the trees overlooking the dawn of another wintry day in Greenville. The sun blazed through a gap in the dense grey clouds rolling in from the west, no doubt bringing another fresh fall of snow. From my vantage point, Greenville wasn't in need of any more. It piled up beside the Whizzenmog home, which had almost been swallowed whole.

A brisk breeze ruffled the feathers of my face. I spread my wings lifting myself into the air...gliding backward slightly. I pulled my wings in tight and darted back toward the ground. Snow kicked up behind me as I zoomed across it. Flying was exhilarating. I loved to move through the air as an eagle. I so rarely had the opportunity to enjoy this form as I only came to Greenville when Queen Merran requested. Since Phillip Harper and the Whizzenmog twins had returned from Mistasia, I had personally come back to Greenville on only a few occasions. The Queen usually sent others, but today she had honored me with this request... to provide protection for the heroes of Mistasia, Phillip, Rachel and Whizzy.

The window to Whizzy's room was empty as I swooped past. I fully expected him to be sleeping in bed as Rachel was when I passed hers. It was still early morning in Greenville and time seemed to be crawling. I would only be remaining here until the twins had awoken.

I settled into another tree that allowed me to watch Rachel. It was good to see her again. I felt a smile, just as a snapping sound startled me from below. My wings opened, and I launched myself toward the noise. It was still shrouded in darkness as the Whizzenmog's house blocked the morning sunlight from the world far below the tree tops.

Wind whistled across my face. I felt freedom like I could never imagine as an elf back home in Mistasia. Swooping into the darkness, my keen eyes quickly adjusted to the lack of light. A figure came into focus, hunched at the base of a tree...its back facing me.

I yelled out, "Don't move!"

The figure dashed away.

I angled to the right and followed the slender creature between the trees. It tossed acorns over its shoulders like grenades in an attempt to stop my pursuit, but I persisted. It was my duty from the queen to protect the twins from any assailants while they slept...and I refused to fail.

I quickly gained on the scurrying foe zipping between the trees and shrubs for cover. Up ahead it was trapped. I landed hemming my furry enemy in.

"Give up!" I shouted raising my wings in a threatening manner.

"AHHHHHH!!" screamed the ugly beast in a high pitched squeal. "Don't hurt me."

"What are you doing here?"

"I'm gathering nuts."

That wasn't quite the answer that I was expecting. It clearly became apparent that this creature was quite afraid of me as its bushy tail vigorously whipped around.

"Who sent you?" I eagerly pressed.

"My wife. She was really mad because I had friends over last night, and we ate the last of our winter nuts."

"What?" I knew that at some point I would encounter a creature that spoke in a language unfamiliar to me. This filthy looking one was it. "So you weren't sneaking up on the Whizzenmog twins?"

"Who?" It replied nervously.

"Yes!" I had a sudden realization. This creature was so small and daring it had gone unnoticed, even to me, until it made a vital mistake by snapping a twig. "LaCroiux believed he could deceive me."

"Who?" my foe questioned again, slightly shaking.

"What are you? A ferret from the Eastern Plains?"

"No...I'm a squirrel...from that tree." He pointed behind me to a thick, tall specimen that had a whole carved in its base.

"A squirrel? Are you sure you're not a ferret?" I questioned him.

"Yes?" He replied.

"And you don't know the Whizzenmogs"

"No."

A gust of wind rushed between the trees sending snow into my face. The squirrel used the opportunity to dash away and into its home.

Upon my return to the Whizzenmogs, I discovered my duty had been fulfilled. The Whizzenmog twins had awoken, and both now sat at their dining room table. I felt pride in seeing them safe, but sad too that I would again have to leave. I would not know when I would get to see them again.

I had returned to Mistasia and returned to my duties for the Queen. Later that night, I was restless...unable to sleep. I stepped up to my window and unlocked the shutters. Outside Cadieux Castle, the wind howled ferociously, sounding the charge of Mistasia's latest wintry blast. It rushed against my fair-skinned cheeks turning them a rosy red. My eyes watered from its sting, yet I remained standing there defiantly studying every cascading wave of snow, like a force of enemy soldiers attacking us. I felt hatred for each and every flake of snow that invaded the castle. A powerful gust pushed a wave of snow in through my window against my face. I ducked and covered. The snow pushed me backward. I braced myself quickly in order to keep from falling.

This is no ordinary snow, I perceived after watching it for nearly an hour. **There is something more sinister on these winds than Mistasia would bring alone.**

The small village just outside of the castle grounds wasn't even visible through the white wall of snow. Drifts crawled up the walls inching closer to the window just outside my room. I stared it down as though it were an approaching Wolverine soldier. I was not going to allow it to enter the castle.

I must protect the Queen.

My charge was to guard the Queen and lead the Elven Warriors in protecting this castle and its lands. Yet, I felt helpless against the advancing winter storm. Watching it slowly work to trap us inside. I grew frustrated.

I couldn't recall a winter this tough in all my life. The snow had been falling for days. The air was brisk and relentless as it cut through my window, swept out the door and rumbled down the hallway.

I just wanted to battle the storm. My hand rested eagerly on the hilt of my sword. I hadn't used it much of late. There had been no need. The storm had deterred even our most stubborn enemies from venturing out. I wished for action...adventure, and I needed it soon.

I would regret those wishes sooner than I could have ever imagined.

DO DREAMS COME TRUE

2

I released a deep sigh. **This storm couldn't last forever, I** hoped. A faint sound fell to my keen ears. **Who would be walking the castle at this time of night? All should be asleep and the guards posted at the main entrances.**

I yanked my sword free and spun to face my attacker.

"You know, a healer could make you a potion to cure your jitters." Standing just outside my doorway unfazed by my brazen attempt to protect myself was my long-time friend, Mecca Begron. He smiled widely quite amused by me aggressively pointing my sword in his direction. I had to look ridiculous. "We don't want you to go stabbing the maid...accidently of course."

"Shut up, Mecca," I barked feeling embarrassed and annoyed. I wished it had been some assailant sent to attack me. I needed the practice. For a moment, I thought about smacking him in the face with the blunt side of my blade just to cure his sarcasm, but it was one of his very few redeeming qualities.

Instead, I stowed my sword at my side and turned back to face the quickly darkening view out my window. Many of the torches around the castle had succumb to the winds and been extinguished.

I rested my thin fingers upon the icy-cold stone window sill. A shiver flowed up my hands, through my arms and into my body. It set in deeply, nearly to the bone. This winter was affecting me more severely than any before.

"Persistent isn't it?" Mecca groaned as he now stood beside me. His smile was gone. It had been replaced by concern.

I didn't respond, nor did I need too. Mecca knew what I was thinking. We had been friends since childhood. We had developed a unique sense of one another's emotions. He was very aware of how restless I had become lately.

"Do you feel that?" I asked.

"Yah, it's really cold," Mecca jokingly replied as the wind burst into the room and ruffled his jacket. He pulled it closed again.

I frowned. My white-hair flowed with the stiff breeze catching Mecca's attention. I normally wore it pulled back and tied away from my face.

He reached out and pushed it away from my shoulder.

I shot him a disapproving glare. Mecca shook his head and gave a half-smile as he scoffed at me.

"You know, this is why you don't have any friends, Grace."

"You're my friend, Mecca."

"Ah, yes, I am."

I was confused by his response. He didn't sound so sure.

"What did that mean?"

"Well, I have known you for a long time. I've grown to understand you."

"Understand me?" I had a feeling I wasn't going to like the response to my latest question.

"Grace," Mecca started to become uncomfortable.

"What, Mecca? Understand me how?"

"You're just not...friendly toward others. You make them all...scared."

"Scared? But, my job is to protect them! Why would they be scared of me?" I suddenly realized that I was yelling, as Mecca put his hands out in an attempt to defend himself from my verbal attack.

We remained silent for a moment as I stewed in my anger. The wind continued to howl through the open window. My cheeks were now on fire from the burn, and my ears began to ache.

"You did pull a sword on me earlier," Mecca spoke softly.

A smile crept upon my face. "I'm sorry about that. I have just been on edge lately."

Mecca began to chuckle. His laughter grew with each second until it had become unruly. It was one of the greatest sounds in Mistasia. His laugh could change the mood of an entire hall. Elves would flock to him when he began to tell stories, because they knew he would start laughing at some point. It was infectious. It was why he had ascended to my second in command. He was a warrior they followed out of respect and admiration. I was the leader they feared, mostly because I had a tendency to pull out weapons for no apparent reason...like tonight.

He placed one arm around my shoulder, then reached out and closed the shutters upon my window. His strong arm pulled me in close. Mecca was like a brother to me.

"Grace, everyone respects you."

"They love you, Mecca."

"You are our leader. They don't have to love you. They must follow you." Mecca pulled me in as closely as possible. He stood nearly a full head taller than me with thick blonde hair and a strong jaw. He was smiling again. Mecca was never short on smiles.

I, on the other hand, was never short on worry; about the queen, about protecting the castle, about Mistasia, and most recently about my new friend, Michael "Whizzy" Whizzenmog. It had been sometime since he had returned to his world along with his twin sister, Rachel, and best friend Phillip Harper, but suddenly his image haunted me. It was one of the many reasons why I hadn't been sleeping. I had gladly accepted the queen's request to monitor them in Greenville last night, but it hadn't helped my mood any. Only a few hours of sleep a day will do that to you.

"You need some rest, Grace. That is all." Mecca attempted to comfort me.

I shook free of his grasp. "I've tried." I grumbled after moving to sit atop my bed.

Mecca sat beside me, the look of concern had returned to his face. It was not his best look. I preferred his smile.

"What is keeping you awake? Nightmares?"

I nodded, but felt silly replying.

"It's the fox again." Mecca's voice grew stern.

Mecca disapproved of my friendship with Whizzy. I started to walk away, but he grabbed my arm and pulled me back.

"Stop walking away from me, Grace."

"I'm not talking to you about it!" I barked.

"Then who will you tell? I'm your only friend!"

He instantly regretted those words. I could see it in his eyes, but my anger flowed too quickly. I shot up from the bed and screamed at him, "GET OUT!" I pointed to the doorway with one hand and grabbed the hilt of my sword with the other. "You know I'll use it."

Mecca stopped in the doorway with his back to me, "I'm sorry."

"Sorry for what, Mecca? Hurting my feelings?"

Mecca started to speak when I interrupted him.

"You're not my only friend, Mecca."

"Whizzy will bring you only pain, Grace."

"Good night!" I slammed the heavy wooden door.

I began pacing across the floor, fists balled in anger at my side. I had taken my sword off to avoid any unfortunate incidents...actually, I was afraid Mecca would return to apologize, and I would jab him with it.

There was a knock at my door. I stopped pacing and stared at the closed door flabbergasted. **Twice in one night he comes to my door. Mecca, so help me.** I looked at the sword lying across my bed and thought better of retrieving it. Instead, I opened the door unarmed.

To my surprise, standing there was Queen Merran Cadieux.

QUEEN'S PLEA

3

"My queen, what are you doing here? And without guards?" I scolded as I quickly ushered her into the room and closed the door tightly.

The young Elven Queen, Merran Cadieux, wore an impish grin as she always did when I fretted about her safety. There had been no attempts upon her life since the defeat of her uncle, Cragon Cadieux, and I planned to keep it that way. She was used to my overzealous efforts to keep her safe, and I had grown used to her regal smile and effortless dismissal of my brash tone of voice. No one else in Mistasia would be allowed to act this way in front of her, but I had been her guardian since she was an infant and that gave me some liberties.

The queen bowed slightly, once I had calmed down enough to address her properly. I bowed back respectfully. Queen Merran had arrived at a very peculiar time and with an ever-increasing smile.

She must have something important to tell me, I believed. It had to be important for her to travel the castle alone...and at night. She had been wary of nightfall since an early age.

"I gave strict orders for the guards to remain with you at all times, my Queen." I felt a sudden swell of anger and dishonor for allowing her to walk unprotected through the castle.

"Yes, Grace, I understand, but needed to dismiss them after two attempted to join me in the royal bathroom."

I felt myself staring at the queen. What exactly was she getting at?

"You do realize I would enjoy some privacy?" the queen smiled.

Her smile made me irritated. She could smile at almost any situation. How the heck was someone who had lost her parents so happy all the time?

"But they are just protecting you, my Queen."

"From what exactly...robbers in the potty?" Her voice sounded less friendly, more disappointed.

"But, I…" I began to defend myself when she put her hand up to stop me.

"That is not why I'm here, Grace." A smile returned to her rosy face. "My parents are alive!" She squealed.

"What!" I screamed, startling her. "That's impossible." I whispered, barely allowing the words to escape my lips, but she heard them anyway.

I've received word otherwise from the Outer Realm. The queen answered using our Elven telepathy. She could barely contain her happiness. It beamed from her face. I couldn't blame her. She could barely remember their faces. She was so young when they had been betrayed by her uncle, the very same elf who was currently imprisoned in the castle dungeon…frozen in time. The very thought of seeing her parents alive again must have become overwhelming. If she wasn't the queen, she would probably be crying with joy, but she had spent her whole life controlling her emotions.

I opened the door, searching for eavesdroppers in the hallway before securing the door and checking the lock multiple times. I worried that anyone who heard this conversation would claim the queen had gone insane and become unfit to rule.

"That is impossible, Merran." I empathically responded. "I tell you this as a friend."

"Do you? I would believe a friend would be more encouraging and less heartless, Grace."

"Heartless? Does the truth make me heartless? You would prefer I lie to you with a smile, my Queen?" I snarked. I was quite glad that my sword still lay upon my bed away from my reach at this moment. I felt naked without it. I was useless in a war of words, especially against someone so well trained as Queen Merran; therefore, I am fairly certain I would have drawn it out by this point.

The room had grown awkwardly silent. She saw me glance at my sword. Her bottom lip began to quiver. She was breaking down.

I was shocked to watch her crumbling before me.

"You, of all people, Grace, should know what this would mean to Mistasia." She began to sob. "...And to me."

It had been so very long since I had seen her cry, not since that horrific day when her parents disappeared. The day the castle fell to her uncle's rule so long ago.

That was until Whizzy arrived with his friend, Phillip the Frog, and sister, Rachel. They turned the tide and freed us from Merran's uncle. It was the reason why she was queen and Cragon was imprisoned in ice.

A smile formed on my face, as I had images of Whizzy on my mind. I had become lost in my own head.

"You find pleasure in my pain? You are not the friend I once believed you to be, Grace Tallon." The queen managed to speak through her tears. "I came to you, not because you are my guardian but because you were my friend."

My smile quickly disappeared, "I am your friend, Merran."

"I need to know if it is true. If they are alive." The young Elven Queen pleaded with me. I could see the pain in her eyes. It was so much deeper than I had ever known.

"What do you need from me?" I asked stepping to her as the guardian of a queen should.

"I have received word from the Outer Realm that my parents are being held captive in the Deadly…"

"…Spray Forest." I finished with her.

The Deadly Spray Forest was a place that had long been avoided by the Elves of Mistasia. Trolls, Vampire bats and many other terrible creatures were held within. It was far more dangerous than Wolverine Forest and the trees were believed to be toxic...and alive.

What could have taken them in there? I wondered. That thought alone frightened me.

"I need you to travel to the Outer Realm and rendezvous with Delza Yorne. She is the village guardian and will be able to guide you to the forest."

I nodded. Our eyes met. Queen Merran's sorrow waned as an intense determination had returned to her gaze.

"Grace, please, be careful."

I wrapped a thick woolen cover around me, tying it firmly across my waist to protect against the chill of winter's wind, and stepped out into the courtyard. Drifts of snow crawled up the castle walls along either side of me. The wind howled between the towers. I pulled my hood up to cover my stinging ears.

This trip could be treacherous on the best of days, but in the heart of Mistasian winter this trip would become deadly in a matter of moments. I couldn't do this alone, but only trusted one other to accompany me in this journey...Mecca.

He awaited me at my modest home along the edge of Cadieux Village. My best friend huddled from the cold, standing beside the majestic, broad-backed steed, Millessa, that would take us upon our journey. She was tall and strong, muscles bulging from her well defined limbs. Millessa had long been a key warrior in our battles against the evils of Mistasia.

I stroked her snout. She rarely spoke and tonight was no different. I felt her willingness and steadied resolve. Millessa was ready.

"Are you going to explain exactly why we are freezing to death instead of resting comfortably in the castle?" Mecca groaned. His usually happy demeanor was as distant as our final destination. I wasn't sure if it was because of our recent argument or the terrible weather.

I smiled. It hurt my cheeks. "We have a quest." I answered hoping to find a reaction, but the cold froze it within him. Mecca had no intention of wasting energy; he knew this was going to be an exhausting journey.

"Then we best be on our way." Mecca mounted Millessa, and stretched out his hand for me.

"We need Fraydorn."

"A second steed? Millessa is more than capable of carrying us both, Grace." Mecca replied.

"Our quest is to return with the king and queen," I revealed.

The expression upon Mecca's face was everything I expected. Confusion combined with a deep worry for my sanity.

"Fraydorn will be bringing home our lost royals...according to Queen Merran." I couldn't believe that I was speaking these words aloud to another living soul. I turned away from Mecca to avoid his glare.

"Sounds as though our queen has been sipping from the fountains of desperation," Millessa spoke in a deep feminine voice.

My Elven friend chuckled as he pulled his thick black woolen coat under his chin. His head buried under a hood, cheeks red from the wind. It gave him a sinister appearance, except for the light-hearted grin.

"Grace," he called to me.

I had started around my house to retrieve Fraydorn. Millessa followed like the faithful steed she had always been. Mecca watched me from her back, awaiting my reply.

I gave none.

Mecca tried again to gather my attention. "Grace, do you believe in this quest?"

I stopped walking and turned slightly. I could just make out his shadow in the dim moonlight from the corner of my eye.

"Well, do you?" He pressed.

Millessa's eyes were drawn to me. Her beautiful white coat glistened from the snowflakes that had melted upon her.

"I believe in our queen," I solemnly replied then started off again.

THUD! Mecca had leapt from Millessa's back, sprung into the air, flipped over my head and landed before me on the frozen trail. He placed his hands firmly upon my shoulders. That famous smile beamed from his face.

"And I believe in you, Grace," He empathically announced.

Millessa snorted.

Mecca glanced over at her.

"Elves," she spat crassly.

"Do you mind? I am trying to let my friend know that I'm with her until the end."

I swatted his hands free and barked, "You have no choice, Mecca. The queen has given me this quest, and I commanded that you accompany me. Now mount your horse and wait here for me to return."

I stomped off, mumbling under my breath about how irritating and annoying my friend had become. **Right now, I would prefer to be with my traitorous brother**, I muttered.

"Now, that's not very nice, Grace," my knuckle-headed friend replied.

Mecca, if you don't stay out of my head...I'll feed you to the first dragon that flies into our path. "Sometimes telepathy is a curse." I scoffed.

We rode out of Cadieux Village under the cover of darkness in order to avoid being noticed. It would be the talk of the town if the queen's two highest ranking guardians scrambled out of the castle in the dead of winter.

A slivered, crescent-shaped moon dangled in the sky, accompanied by its minions, millions of stars. The breeze had subsided lending to warmth under my woolen coat as we rumbled along the shore of Red River. Our journey would take a few days to reach the Outer Realm, the most northern Elven village in Mistasia.

Mecca pushed Millessa hard, forcing her to pull up alongside Fraydorn and me. We galloped side-by-side for many miles without speaking. He would glance my way occasionally awaiting me to speak, but I refused. There was nothing to say...for now.

ARROWS UPON US

4

I awoke to the sounds of rustling. Springing to my feet, I loaded an arrow into my bow, pulled back its string and aimed.

"I almost shot you through the heart!" I barked with irritation at Mecca, who stood beside a jittery Millessa, as he rearranged items in her side pack.

"I've grown used to you pointing deadly weapons at me," he replied with a snort. "You haven't harmed me yet." He had pulled a large green apple from Millessa's side pouch and fed it to her before reaching back in and grabbing another.

I let loose my arrow, piercing the apple dead center, ripping it from his thick fingers and pinning it against the tree which we took shelter underneath.

"Hey," Mecca protested as Fraydorn whinnied with glee. Fraydorn always enjoyed it when I taunted and tortured Mecca.

"That was my breakfast...and what are you laughing at, horse face?"

The large golden-brown steed was slightly bigger than his sister, Millessa, and son to the royal horses that transported Queen Merran Cadieux's parents long ago. It was why I had chosen him for this journey even though his coat would be obvious in the white-wash of this snow covered landscape, except for the haven of Blue Elm that we currently used as cover. These sturdy trees had grown accustomed to the long harsh winters of Mistasia and nearly retained all of their deep blue leaves throughout.

Fraydorn was the strongest and most exceptional steed in the Cadieux family line, bred for endurance. Millessa was my usual steed and the bravest of them all, despite what her brother may claim. She had fought many a troll, wolverine and dragon in battle with me defending the castle. For this journey, I had chosen to ride Fraydorn instead, simply because of my elven company. Mecca and Fraydorn didn't exactly get along.

Their squabble had begun a few years ago during battle, when Fraydorn claimed Mecca...well, how did he explain it?

"The elf deadened my senses with his bottom bomb," Fraydorn recalled with his sister as Mecca roared with laughter at her side. Millessa joined him for a moment until her brother shot her a stern look. The uptight steed huffed with offense.

"I told you I had just eaten a spicy mushroom when those darn trolls attacked. All that bouncing around...it got me stirred up on the inside. You shouldn't have been jumping around so much Fraydorn," Mecca could barely finish his sentence as he laughed harder with each passing moment.

"You blame me? I heard you ate them on purpose, Elf!" Fraydorn scolded.

"How was I to know those darn beasts would attack? Besides, Grace fed them to me." Mecca pointed in my direction to pass the blame, his eyes wide, tight lipped and attempting not to explode into laughter.

"I did not!" I shouted in defense. "Those mushrooms were on the table for my stew. I hadn't even cooked them yet."

"Oh, really?" Fraydorn moved closer to my friend, attempting to intimidate Mecca.

"That's why his gas was so potent, Fraydorn. He ate them fresh."

The golden-brown steed stuck his snout in Mecca's face. The Elven warrior's laughter returned.

"As I recall Mecca, you shoved about four large mushrooms in your mouth as we dashed out to battle. You said something about blowing up a few trolls with a 'riot of explosion'"

Everyone wailed, except Fraydorn; he was far too uptight for potty humor. Mecca did much of what he did to irritate Fraydorn...and me for that matter. At least this time his nonsense was directed upon someone else.

The sun had begun to set and we needed to move. Night time was the best chance for us to travel without being noticed by the terrors of Mistasia.

We were approximately one night's ride from the Outer Realm now. Our journey had been uneventful, which made me edgy. Mecca, as usual, had found a way to relax my tension, even if for only a few moments.

I led us from the cluster of Blue Elm trees that had served as our protection throughout the past day and into the vast open space between us and the Outer Realm. Being Elf gave me an advantage in these wild lands. I could see quite clearly even in the dark. My keen ears also allowed me to hear any enemies that might be attempting to sneak up on us...I just needed to remain focused.

However, my mind began to race, eyes searching the area for any movement that could provide signs that someone was out there. A pressure gathered between my eyes. My instincts were at the verge of cracking under the strain. I was worried about our safety but fearful of what we just might find when we reached the Deadly Spray Forest. **Would we really find King Stephan and his wife, Delia? Would they really be alive, trapped in the forest?**

Grace! A voice shouted in my head, startling me awake from my dream. **What is that?** Mecca's voice sounded unusually surprised.

Ahead of us, in the darkness, colors swirled in the sky. It cast shadows over the silhouetted image of the Outer Realm. We were almost there, yet after these past few days of hard travel, I had the sudden urge to turn around and head back to Cadieux Castle.

Grace, what in Mistasia is that?

I have no idea. I replied keeping the conversation between us Elves.

The wind pushed hard against my face flinging my hood back, exposing me ears to the harsh cold. Snow lifted from the ground, swept skyward by the winds. Fraydorn struggled against the powerful gusts.

We slowly approached the village along the Red River. The slender-crescent moon was all the light that showed our way, and it had nearly been blotted out by the snow.

Where did this snowfall come from? Mecca groaned as he rode up beside me.

"It's not snowing, Mecca. The snow is being pulled skyward by whatever that is above the village." I stared blankly at the violently swirling lines of blue, green and yellow light.

The wind suddenly stopped. All sounds vanished like a void. A stiff pressure filled my ears. Mecca's too, I could tell as he covered them with his hands. The colorful light flashed toward the ground and exploded tearing apart a series of small buildings. Fraydorn knelt down bracing for the sonic boom. It swept in from the village knocking Millessa back tossing Mecca to the snow.

I dismounted and rushed to Mecca's aid. My ears numbed from the blast, it took a moment to understand the noise coming from my friend, but I should have known...he was laughing.

"I'm fine," he chuckled. "Help me up."

Our horses had moved behind us allowing a full view of the village smoldering. Flames danced atop the blackened remains of the buildings that had just stood there moments earlier. The colorful storm above had mysteriously vanished too.

Dread filled my body. Fear began to invade my mind with full force. Every part of me body ached. I desperately wanted to turn and leave but was too embarrassed to admit it. **I am Grace Tallon, Elven Warrior and Guardian to the Queen.** That is what I said to myself attempting to reassure my mind.

"What was that, Grace?" Fraydorn asked.

I shook my head. I had no response.

"It wasn't a storm of nature. That's for darn sure." Mecca brushed snow from his woolen coat.

My heart thumped hard in my head. I was regretting coming on the quest and we hadn't even made it to our initial destination yet.

A familiar sound rang out in my wind-burnt ears. The sound of steel sliding from its home, Mecca had unsheathed his sword.

"I'm not going in there unprepared," Mecca announced.

"That sounds unfair. I can't hold a sword," Fraydorn whined.

"Just use your tongue."

I pulled my sword free and gripped the hilt tightly in my cold fingers. "Mecca!" I barked.

"Yeah?"

"Shut it!" I moved ahead, trudging one foot at a time through the thickening snow. The top layer was fresh and powdery, yet below it was crusty and hardened. Snow was past my knees in areas and quickly rising near my hips. Travel had become increasingly difficult.

We entered the village of the Outer Realm with great apprehension. Lit by the bright moonlight from above and the smoldering flames where much of the village once stood. A few small buildings remained, but those too had cracked and scorched walls.

A rustling noise emerged from a badly burnt building to my right. A rush of wind hit my face; it carried a familiar sound...an arrow. I swung my blade deflecting the arrow just enough that it only grazed my shoulder, tearing through my jacket. Standing in the doorway was a figure. A glint of light sparkled from the tip of another arrow pointed directly at me. Two ferocious eyes gazed upon me.

"Show yourself!" I commanded.

It let loose another arrow.

Mecca cut it in half before it could reach me. The arrows pieces dove into the snow at my feet.

"By order of the queen's guards...show yourself! Now!" Mecca barked.

I reached for my bow and arrow and aimed at the shadowed figure. I watched as it slowly emerged from the building into the moonlight. It wore a hood to cover its face.

"I will not warn you again. Show yourself!" I shouted with my arrow pointed at it.

The figure reached up and removed its hood.

OUTER REALM

5

Standing before us was a young elf, she was beautiful yet angry. Her intense, golden eyes darted between us with contempt. She appeared to be searching our minds for answers...if we were friends or foes. Her flowing, brunette hair flapped in the blustery winds.

I quickly commandeered her attention with arrow still raised. I needed to know why she tried to kill me...an elf like her.

"We do not harm our own kind without good reason." I raised an eyebrow in contempt.

She shot me a horrific stare. "Nor do we leave our own to perish alone," she spat.

I quickly lowered my arrow and released the tension on my bow. "No, we do not." I replied.

"Who has been attacking this village?" Mecca interjected as he witnessed the devastation.

"The sorcerer." She replied with furrowed brow. She quickly approached. "And you Commander Tallon have abandoned us. Where is your honor?" The young girl hissed.

Mecca grabbed her by the arm, and she kicked out his legs, knocking him to the snow. She removed her sword reached back and stopped mid swing. My arrow was only a few inches from her nose; once again I was ready to fire.

"Put down the sword." I calmly commanded. "I think you are misguided young one. Your anger is just, but directed improperly at me when it should be toward the one that brought this chaos to the Outer Realm." We stared at one another with unwavering resolve. "Tell me of this sorcerer. What is his name?"

"LaCroiux."

I felt a shiver run through my body. I quickly lowered my weapon, gazing at Mecca who shared my fearful expression. Sorcerer LaCroiux had returned. That meant awful things to more than just the Outer Realm in Mistasia.

She led us into the burnt building and through the charred remains of the home it once was...her home, Delza Yorne. She was the elf that Queen Merran had asked us to find here. Delza was to take us to the Deadly Spray Forest to find the lost King and Queen of Mistasia. We never expected to find this upon our arrival.

Delza took us briskly into a narrow passage that dipped below the floor and led through a dirt-walled tunnel that spiraled down into the depths below the village. At the bottom of the tunnel was a heavy wooden door. She knocked and awaited a response from within. After her coded reply, which neither Mecca nor I understood as any current form of Elfish language, the door slowly retreated. Inside was an underground world far more intricate than that beneath Cadieux Castle, and it was full of Elves.

"What is this place, Delza?" I asked.

"The Outer Realm has long been the furthest Elven village away from the castle. We learned long ago that we must protect ourselves from the beasts of Mistasia. This underground shelter provided us that protection from LaCroiux when you didn't." Delza's words stabbed at me.

"I had no idea that your village was under attack...that our people were in danger."

"Communication has been cut off for some time now. I hoped that you would have noticed and sent warriors to check up on us in the very least, Commander Tallon." Delza handed her sword to an elderly elf. "Please repair the edges, Elder Smorg.

He nodded and hobbled off to a work station nearby. Instantly, he set to work sharpening the edge of Delza's blade along a large stone wheel.

"I am sorry, Delza." I began when I was rudely interrupted.

"Chief Yorne," She brashly replied looking at me intensely.

I stopped in shock.

"Chief? Who named you chief?" Mecca mocked.

"The people of the Outer Realm," She soundly retorted. "When it became apparent that our Commander had abandoned us...they named me Chief Commanding Officer overseeing the village and its protection." Delza left, leaving Mecca and I standing alone.

"What is going on here?" I mumbled in frustration.

"Well, it appears that you can add Chief Yorne to the "*not-a-friend*" list," Mecca mocked.

"This isn't funny, Mecca." I watched as a group of villagers had gathered around Chief Yorne. They muttered and pointed in our direction with looks of disdain and hatred on their faces.

"She has turned them against us."

"How are we going to get her to help us?" Mecca questioned.

"That will be simple. She may be '*Chief* of the Outer Realm,' but she still is under the control of the Queen of Mistasia."

Day broke shortly after we had descended into the world under the Outer Realm. We would have to wait for nightfall again before we could venture out for the forest. There was little cover in the light of day between this Elven realm and the horrors of the Deadly Spray Forest.

I had grown eager and impatient, which was why I stood alone in the burnt out home of Chief Yorne peering through a hole in the wall at our objective in the distance. The trees in the

Deadly Spray Forest were menacingly tall with branches that hung down like the tentacles of an octopus. They swayed in the wind as though dancing on the horizon, taunting me…laughing at my fear. Horrible creatures lived in that forest; trolls, vampire bats, and now apparently a sorcerer. It would make sense that LaCroiux had made this forest his home. He once lived in Wolverine Forest, but unable to head back there, he found a new place…one with far more hideous creatures to control. From there he could easily attack this village, without even leaving the safety of the trees.

The chill of the air had set into my bones. My breath was exposed as the warm air from my lungs turned to thick white puffs in the freezing air outside. I rubbed my hands together in a vain attempt for warmth. It lasted only a few seconds.

"Grace?" Mecca's voice called from the tunnel behind me. He wasn't alone. Chief Yorne walked beside him. They appeared to be in the middle of a conversation…a civil conversation. Mecca did have a way with elves…especially females. His smile entered the room first. I smiled back…I just couldn't help it. That seemed to catch Chief Yorne by surprise. She gave a forced smile in return and slightly bowed. I did as well out of courtesy, not respect.

The sun had begun to set. The sky was a brilliant array of colors; from pink to orange to purple.

"Chief Yorne, we will be leaving shortly." I paused for a moment wondering how exactly to broach the subject of her leading us to the Deadly Spray Forest.

"Please, call me Delza. I apologize for how I behaved earlier. I should not have shown you such disrespect."

"I understand, Delza. You and your people have been through a great deal. I am sorry."

"I will gather my belongings and be prepared to assist you, Commander Tallon. Mecca has informed me of our mission...ah 'quest'." She corrected as she turned to Mecca for reassurance. "At Queen Merran's request, I will accompany you to the forest." The Chief nodded again and left.

Mecca and I stood alone in the cold. It was silent. Mecca's smile was beaming brighter than the sunset.

"Come on, Grace; you can say it."

"Say what?"

"How good I am."

I chuckled. "Yeah, you're good alright. Now go get our friends."

"What would you do without me?" Mecca joked.

"Yes, Mecca I am glad you're here," I regretfully replied. He most certainly didn't need his ego stroked any further. His head might grow so large that he would fall over.

After he left the room, I returned my gaze upon the horizon. I exhaled deeply. The pit in my stomach grew heavier.

"But you, my friend, may soon not be."

I sat tall upon Fraydorn's back while Delza climbed up Millessa to join Mecca. Tightening the strap that held my sword, I inhaled sharply. The rush of cold air stabbed my lungs.

"Grace? Are you alright?" Mecca noticed my discomfort.

I nodded, but my chest still hurt. Shaking it off, I grabbed Fraydorn by the reigns and pulled tightly. He lurched into the air and roared. We were off into the darkness.

Just outside the village the winds began to intensify. Snow formed a wall before us, encircling us.

A tornado! Delza called out with telepathy.

She was correct. The snow whipped around us.

"Ahhhhh!" I yelled as Fraydorn charged into the vortex. I was knocked clear from his back in an instant. I heard Fraydorn's voice call to me as I was whisked away. I landed in a large pile of snow, but the tornado continued to push more on top of my body. It was burying me alive.

Mecca! I called for my friend. There was no answer. The snow kept coming. My legs were buried deep. The wintry wind storm had me pinned down and was now attempting to finish me. I kicked my left leg free, but an angry growl echoed from the tornado as it doused me with a huge wave of white powder. Now, only my face and right arm were free.

A figure suddenly emerged from the swirling winds.

Fraydorn!

He grabbed hold of my arm in his mouth. The sharp pain from his teeth was a small price to pay for my freedom. Fraydorn yanked me loose. Blood trickled down my arm and dotted the white snow. I slung myself onto Fraydorn's back and hunched down to avoid the wind knocking me off again.

Fraydorn burst through the vortex of snow and we were ahead of the roaring monster. Millessa rode up beside us with Mecca and Delza still on her back.

The chilling blast of wintry air kept the pain in my arm from throbbing as we raced ahead of the tornado. I turned back to see just how close it was. In the winds was the face of a monster.

"LaCroiux," I muttered in anger.

Delza noticed too and fired an arrow into his mouth. LaCroiux swallowed it and spat it back at her, narrowly missing. The tornado cackled as it chased us down. There was nowhere to go. We were easy prey for the sorcerer out in the open fields.

Suddenly, I realized our fate. LaCroiux knew that I wouldn't dare return to the village of innocent elves. The only choice would be to enter the Deadly Spray Forest for shelter. He was driving us right toward him. We ran directly for his trap.

DEADLY FOREST

6

The roar of the wind trampled the snow behind us like thousands of horses charging into battle...with us.

The Deadly Spray Forest sprawled out before us. The power from the tornado pulled the tree branches like arms reaching out to snatch us. It was a frightening sight.

LaCroiux cackled heartily, signaling his latest attack. I turned around to witness arms forming at the tornado's side. They swirled around above his head gathering tremendous speed. Then LaCroiux whipped them toward us.

The first snap landed between Fraydorn and Millessa. The second barely missed Millessa, sending a cascade of snow up across her back. Delza slipped, but Mecca grabbed her at the last second keeping her from falling into the tornado's vortex. Millessa bolted ahead of Fraydorn and me, kicking up a trail of powder in our faces.

We had almost reached the forest when the tornado vanished.

"It's gone!" Delza yelled.

Millessa skidded to a stop and turned to watch the sky clear. Fraydorn galloped up beside.

"Where did he go?" Mecca questioned, slightly out of breath.

"Is he gone?" Delza nervously inquired. She knew the answer though. LaCroiux had been attacking her village for months. It was a false hope that he had given up.

"No! LaCroiux will return. He always returns." I patted Fraydorn as he restlessly moved about. "We must enter the forest."

"I'm not going in there. We don't go into the Deadly Spray Forest," Delza was obviously concerned.

"What is that?" Mecca pointed into the darkness.

I squinted to look through the night. In the distance loomed a wall of snow barreling directly toward us.

"Move!" I shouted pulling on the reins and directing Fraydorn toward the forest.

The noise was terrible as the wall of snow closed in on us quickly.

"It's gaining on us!" Delza screamed.

It was the last words any of us would utter before the snow cascaded over us, pushing us into the forest. I was pulled free from Fraydorn. I tumbled through the snow unable to break free from its grip. Finally, I skidded to a stop, much of my body buried in snow. My eyes fluttered. It was so difficult to keep them open. My head throbbed. I searched the area for my friends, but dizziness overtook me. I grew ill and vomited upon the dirty snow, which was tainted by leaves, rocks, sticks and dirt. I couldn't stay awake. I felt my body slump into the snow around me and everything went black.

Grace? Grace can you hear me? Mecca's voice echoed in my head. **Open your eyes.**

I could feel the touch of his strong hands upon my shoulders. My body was in great discomfort. It took too much effort just to pull open my eyelids. I took a short painful breath.

"Grace, be careful. You may have broken a few ribs. It will be difficult to breathe normally." Mecca explained.

Delza sat beside me tending to a wound on her arm. The gash was nearly closed now. Tears streamed down her face, which showed the result of our entry into the forest. Scratches and cuts were along the side of her face and over her eye.

"Where are we, Mecca?" I mustered up the strength to ask. A pain shot down my side as I shifted to sit up right.

"Grace! Take it easy." Mecca had turned his attention back to helping Delza finish closing the wound on her arm. "We are inside the Deadly Spray Forest. Fortunately, we found a place to hide among the trees. LaCroiux has had Vampire bats out looking for us."

"Where are Millessa and Fraydorn?"

It remained silent. Mecca wouldn't look at me.

"Mecca?"

"They were both unconscious, and too large for me to move on my own. I had to leave them. LaCroiux has them now." He wiped the remaining blood from Delza's arm as she winced in pain.

"I'm sorry, Grace. There just wasn't enough time to save everyone." The sound in his voice was heartbreaking. He wasn't accustomed to failure.

"LaCroiux has grown much stronger than the last time we faced him," I stated.

Mecca turned his attention to me. "We need to check your ribs." He placed his hands upon my side. A pain shot straight up into my chest knocking the air from my lungs. "It doesn't feel as though they are broken, Grace."

"Badly bruised," I replied. "Not much better. It will be nearly impossible for me to use my sword."

"Or your bow," Delza spoke as she leaned her head back against the tree behind her, eyes closed.

"I will have to try. It is far too dangerous in this place for me to walk about unprotected. Even if I just hold my weapon it may keep LaCroiux's monsters off me long enough to escape." I said it but wasn't even confident in those words myself. We were in real danger before our injuries, but now we entered a realm of evil. LaCroiux controlled everything here. We now played on his terms, and by his rules.

"You two have to rest. You'll need your strength...or what you can recover before we move on." Mecca began gathering our weaponry and laying it out before us. "This was all that I could recover from the snow." Two bows, a dozen arrows, three swords and a small dagger.

"It will have to do," I attempted to sound as confident as I could. "We shouldn't venture out during night here. We will have to wait until daylight to help guide us."

"Well, there is one problem." Mecca began. "I believe that it is day time now. It is slightly warmer, and I have witnessed some rays of light coming into the forest when the trees move with the winds. These branches are unlike anything I've ever seen, Grace. They act like a canopy protecting us from the snow and cold harsh winds, yet also block almost all sunlight."

"That would explain the dirt blanket," Delza snarled as she ran her hand along the bare forest floor. "Real comfy!"

Mecca half-smiled at her weak attempt at humor. There seemed to be a bond growing between them.

"It beats sleeping in the snow," I muttered. My clothes were still icy cold from my time beneath the snow. Thankfully, these trees kept the winds at bay. Hopefully, they could help keep Sorcerer LaCroiux's henchmen off our scent too.

"Alright you two, get some rest." Mecca stood up and began walking away.

"What if the Vampire bats find us?" Delza asked the question that weighed heavily on us all...she was just the courageous one to speak it aloud.

"Then we fight with whatever strength we have left." I replied attempting to hide the fear that struggled to escape me.

I lay on the hard ground trying to rest my aching body. It was difficult to remain still, especially my mind. I kept watching the trees swaying sometimes seeing figures in them. Closing my eyes didn't help either. Images of LaCroiux hovering over me entered my mind repeatedly. My eyes would snap open again. It was becoming harder to tell dream from reality.

The next time I opened my eyes I felt different. My pain was numbed. Stretching out I realized that I was no longer an elf...I was again an eagle like when I enter Greenville. I took to the sky and maneuvered up through the trees. It was dark and very cold.

"Greenville?" I said in surprise after finding the Whizzenmog house in the distance. I swooped down and perched in the same tree where I had recently watched Whizzy.

A warm sensation entered my chest as I saw him sleeping in his bed. I watched him through the window for a few moments. It was peaceful...too peaceful.

"I should check on Rachel," I extended my wings and prepared to leap from the branch when a strange light appeared in Whizzy's bedroom.

The white light spun with flashes of gold growing more intense with each swirl. It grew larger by the second...a flash lit up the room. It stunned my sensitive eyes. When my vision returned, I was frightened by what I saw. Sorcerer LaCroiux stood beside Whizzy's bed. I tried to get air born, but my body aches had returned. That was when I realized I was no longer an eagle, but myself again grasping the branch.

LaCroiux turned his gaze upon me. A rumbling laughter exploded through the window, bursting the glass out upon me. The same white light glowed from his mouth and eyes.

"You can't protect him, Grace. You can't even protect yourself!" the sorcerer mocked.

I watched helplessly as LaCroiux stood up tall, arms raised. Flames began to dance in his palms, a ferocious expression upon his face like that of a Wolverine preparing to pounce on its prey. He fired a ball of flames into Whizzy's bed. It exploded, shooting flames out the broken window and against my skin. The heat instead felt like a rush of cold air across my body. I began to tumble from the branch. I was falling to my death when suddenly I awoke.

"WHIZZY!" I screamed.

"Grace!" Mecca yelled snapping me back from the horrible nightmare and into our real-life horror.

Mecca helped Delza to her feet.

My heart was still pounding so hard it hurt my head. I struggled to catch my breath amidst the pain in my badly bruised ribs. I rolled to my side, still unaware of just how much danger we were in. Mecca's strong arms wrapped around me and lifted me up.

I whimpered in pain, but held back the urge to scream. Mecca noticed the tears running down my cheeks. Thankfully, he would believe that it was because of the pain in my body and not in my heart after watching Whizzy being destroyed at the hands of our enemy. I had to tell myself it was a dream. I couldn't have actually been in Greenville. LaCroiux was just torturing me...leading me to believe he had done it.

I heard the familiar sound of a sword ringing as it was unsheathed. Mecca held his sword pointed directly before him.

"Think you can fire your bow?" He asked me.

"I don't know how accurately."

"Well, accuracy is gonna count."

For the first time I got to witness our enemies. In the trees were dozens of Vampire bats seething and drooling. Cracking and growling came from the branches. A tree bent forward causing a Vampire bat to flee. Another loud crack exploded into our hideout, followed by a massive meaty fist. The monstrously tall tree snapped in half and crashed to the ground as three Trolls entered.

"We are in serious trouble!" Delza yelped.

"Well, at least he didn't send four Trolls." Mecca looked at me. "Then we'd be outnumbered," Mecca sarcastically replied.

SORCERY

7

There was a strange pause from our enemies. They were awaiting something...a command perhaps. The Vampire bats would jump from tree to tree, but remained high above us as though watching a sporting event.

The Trolls just glared at us, each seemingly choosing its intended target. I found myself sharing eye contact with the apparent leader of the group. Trolls are slow in just about every aspect; their mind, movement and skills; however, in my current condition it was going to be very difficult to take this creature on alone. The Troll's broad shoulders dipped up and down with each massive breath.

"What are they waiting for?" Mecca barked. He was gripping his sword so tightly that his knuckles were pure white.

"Don't be so eager for this fight." That was normally my stance before battle, but this particular fight was not in our favor...even if we were healthy.

"Delza looks jittery," I said to Mecca

"Yes, I think we all are jittery just about now," He replied.

"What are those bats doing?" Delza nervously asked. She raised her bow toward the tree tops aiming her arrow at multiple targets.

"Don't worry about the bats, Delza," I commanded. "The Trolls will attack first. Those nasty flying beasts are probably here to make certain the dumb Trolls do their jobs."

"I don't wanna be eaten," Delza cried. "I can't go out like this." Blood began to trickle from her nose.

"What in Mistasia are they waiting for?" Mecca barked again as he stepped forward.

"No, Mecca wait...don't," I reached for his arm, but a sharp pain held me back.

"What do you wait for?" He yelled at the Trolls. "If this is the end, then let us begin already."

The lead Troll leaned forward; its face features shifting into something all too recognizable...the face of Sorcerer LaCroiux.

"Then we shall begin, little Elf," The sorcerer sneered.

I gasped. Mecca retreated, and Delza fired her arrow directly at the lead Troll hitting him in the cheek. LaCroiux's face was gone. What returned was the ugly features of the Troll, which growled in agony as the arrow pierced its skin. It raised its giant arm back and swung toward her swatting her into the trees behind us. Mecca and I were now left to face these monstrously powerful Trolls outnumbered.

"NOOOOO!" Mecca screamed with hatred, something very unfamiliar for him even in battle. He raised his sword and dodged a Troll's attempt to squash him.

Dirt escaped from the Troll's hand. Mecca leapt up and disappeared into the cloud of dirt and debris. He emerged running up the mountain of an arm toward the Troll's head.

The other two Trolls thundered around their leader and approached me. Panic coursed through my body. I was still too weak to fight them...so I ran into the heart of the forest.

As I entered the maze of entangled limbs and branches of the Deadly Spray Forest, I heard a great cry of agony followed by a tremendous rumble. The trees shook, the ground buckled and I fell to my knees.

"Mecca!" **Mecca, are you alright?** I called out to him using telepathy.

One down...two to go. He replied with determination.

It was then I mustered up the courage to reenter the fray. I took the deepest breath I could handle, readied my bow and arrow, and launched myself through the branches back into the opening. Lying lifeless was the lead troll. Mecca was now attacking a second. I looked up to find the Vampire bats...they were still there watching and jeering.

I slid to a stop and pulled back upon my bow. My first shot missed badly and worse than that it drew attention to the fact that I had returned. I aimed again, this time striking a troll in the neck. It howled in pain. Mecca dashed forward and slashed at its ankles while sliding underneath the giant creature. This troll joined its slain brother falling upon him in the center of the clearing.

Now only one troll remained. We flanked the ugly beast. The troll swatted at us, flailing about angrily. I could sense its fear. We had destroyed two trolls; he knew he didn't stand a chance.

I heard a rustling noise from behind me. Mecca's face beamed. When I turned, Delza stood just inside the clearing. She looked awful, but was still alive.

"You will pay for that," Delza sneered in an unusual voice.

She no longer had her bow, but brandished a short sword and came charging at me. I deflected her attack with my bow, but she swung again knocking my bow free. I winced in pain, grabbing my side as she continued to slash at me in rage. Her eyes were burning with anger.

"LaCroiux?" I muttered to myself. He had overtaken her mind. Delza was now the sorcerer's prisoner. "This is a new trick sorcerer." I grabbed a branch from the ground and swung. Delza's sword sliced through, cutting the branch in two. "Delza, fight him!"

She reached straight back over her head, sword held high. I kicked her in the chest.

Meanwhile, Mecca finished off the remaining troll. I knew by the heavy thud behind me. All three trolls were now heaped upon one another. My friend strolled over toward me confidently, twirling his sword at his side. He attempted to sheath it when I stopped him.

"You may need that."

Delza lay unconscious sprawled out on the ground; her sword now in my hand. She looked battered and beaten. I only hoped that LaCroiux would now leave her alone.

The forest had grown very quiet; only heavy panting from the Vampire bats above could be heard. My ears began to hurt. Pressure building up inside them pushed all sound out like a void. The branches began to lurch inward toward us at all sides. Then a flash of light burst forth; the tall trees bent backward. Mecca and I were knocked to the ground.

I struggled to my knees. There standing atop the fallen trolls was the sorcerer. His strength was impressive. LaCroiux moved down the troll bodies and stopped just before me.

"Commander," he mockingly bowed, staring at me. "You have done quite well. I never thought, with all your injuries, that your group would have been able to destroy these trolls. I guess I was wrong."

"What have you done with the King and Queen?" I questioned through gritted teeth.

He snorted. "Well, you will be disappointed to know that they are not here."

"Where are they, LaCroiux?" Mecca shouted.

The sorcerer swung his arm, swatting Mecca high up into the air. A Vampire bat clutched him and flew off. Another swooped down and snatched Delza from the ground.

"You are all alone, Grace."

I wasn't about to go out without a fight. I gripped Delza's sword in my right hand.

"You wish to use that against me do you?" LaCroiux snickered. He had always been arrogant. "Do your best." His voice deepened.

I swung, and he dodged effortlessly. Pain shot across my chest. I swung again but missed. LaCroiux punched me in the chest with a spell. I flew through the air, landing on my back. He slowly strolled toward me. I rolled onto my side and struggled with all my might to get back to my knees. I had no strength remaining...at least not enough to fend off a sorcerer.

I swung again, but LaCroiux knocked the sword from my hand and lifted me up into the air with the flick of his wrist. He summoned the winds, which burnt as they swept across my face.

"You are now my prisoner," LaCroiux growled.

A forceful wind lifted me free from his grasp pushing me back until I collided with a tree...everything went black.

EVIL REVEALED

<u>8</u>

"Grace?" LaCroiux's voice echoed in my head. It drifted from ear to ear as though it passed through me.

It was pitch black, not a glimmer of light nor hope. I was Sorcerer LaCroiux's prisoner. I felt a tingling in my body and numbness as my legs were trapped up underneath me. My arms were bound tightly behind my back. My eyes were open, but useless in this prison. I was blind. Fear began to creep its way into my heart.

Where was Mecca? What had happened to my friend? I tried to call to him, but something blocked the sound. It was as though a cloth covered my mouth. There was nothing at all, like something was absorbing it. With my hands bound, I wasn't able to feel what covered my mouth. My lips felt like they were sewn together.

Mecca! I screamed using telepathy. No reply.

Delza! I waited impatiently for any sign from them, but no one answered.

I was all alone. LaCroiux had made sure of that. His torture for me would be solitude. No one would find me here. No Elves would venture into the Deadly Spray Forest...if that's where I was now. LaCroiux could have taken me anywhere.

My mind was overrun with questions.

Where am I?
Why had LaCroiux returned?
Why did he keep me prisoner?
Where was he now?

My heart was pounding like a large drum, echoing off the walls and back to me. The walls must be closing in. They will crush me. Suddenly, a force hit my chest like a Troll's punch slamming me against the wall. A cackling rose above the thundering of my heart.

I attempted to scream, "LaCroiux!" Nothing came out.

The thunder dulled, but was replaced with cold and stars. My stomach flipped as I rose from the ground and floated through the nighttime sky. Horror overtook me. I was weightless, tumbling uncontrollably through nowhere.

The laughter returned. A single dot of light grew before me, the light of a star exploding in space from a million miles away. It began to intensify and with it the sorcerer's laughter grew stronger and louder...the sound of victory. A brilliant flash burned my eyes, which were wide open. I was unable to close them, fixated upon the intense flame.

I screamed in pain as a wave of heat surged across my body. It felt as though my skin was burning away.

Then darkness returned.

I had never left LaCroiux's prison. He was torturing me, turning my own mind and senses against me. No stars, no lights, just darkness and pain. My eyes still stung, legs numbed from the weight of my body pressing down upon them, wrists ached from the binds that tied them together.

I had but one last question. **Why did I still live?**

"That, my dear, is the question." LaCroiux's face emerged in the darkness, shadowed and frightening. His eyes were blazing like the sun.

The sorcerer waved his hand across my face. I was able to open my mouth again. He had removed the spell that had made me unable to speak.

"Set me free, LaCroiux!" I immediately demanded.

LaCroiux laughed. "I don't think so, Commander Tallon. You see, you're a key piece to my game."

"What game?"

"I am playing a political game. You see, I am not completely happy with our current monarch," LaCroiux said.

"Queen Merran? You think that you can replace her on the throne?"

"No, no, no. I am not the ruling type. I prefer to hide in the shadows, place someone else in charge and manipulate them to do my biding." The sorcerer's entire body transformed from the darkness as the nighttime sky returned. He walked before me like a constellation...a God.

"Cragon?" I whispered.

A smile beamed across his face. "Since the former king's untimely departure from the throne, I have grown in my powers. I have used that time to enhance them, and perfect them. Now, I am far more powerful than Cragon Cadieux...this time I will rule through him."

"But the people of Mistasia have their queen!" I shouted in disgust.

"Ah, ah, ah. It would be unwise to speak that way to your new king." LaCroiux slowly waved his fingers in front of my face. I felt my lips tighten and close. He had recast the spell to quiet me. "Grace, the people of Mistasia have no right to decide who is to be their ruler. It is to be decided by whoever is strong enough to claim the throne."

I struggled to free myself, when he pushed me against the wall.

"You were a key acquisition in this plan. Now that I have you, it is time to proceed with the last phase. You will love this part too because it involves someone you hold very dear."

Three figures began to form in the darkness beyond LaCroiux. Fear struck me when I recognized their faces.

"Yes, Phillip Harper and the Whizzenmog twins. I intend to bring them back to Mistasia...using you as bait and then trap them here with you...forever."

THE STORY CONTINUES IN

RETURN TO MISTASIA

THE PHILLIP & WHIZZY TRILOGY (BOOK 2)

www.LandOfMistasia.com

PHILLIP & WHIZZY
TRILOGY

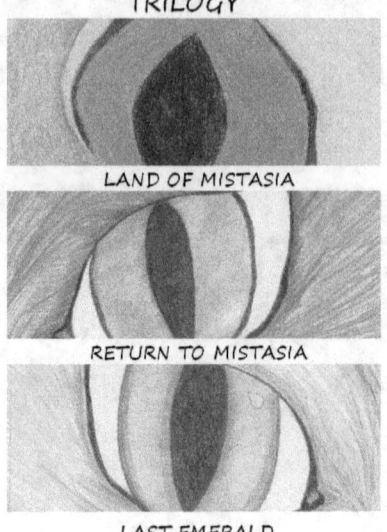

LAND OF MISTASIA

RETURN TO MISTASIA

LAST EMERALD

Available

in

Paperback and Kindle™

www.Amazon.com

Keyword: Mistasia

GOSSAMER PEN COMING FALL 2014
@ PURRETT.COM

FREE WEB COMIC

www.ingramcontent.com/pod-product-compliance
Lightning Source LLC
Chambersburg PA
CBHW070936130626
46555CB00001B/452